W9-BFL-917

An eerie blast on a horn signalled the start of the ceremony and the crowd became silent. The master of ceremonies, in a white, druidical robe, mounted the platform by the launching ramp and stood, peering inland along another path, marked off by ropes which disappeared into the darkness. After a while a flickering light appeared in the distance and drew steadily nearer; a torch-bearer came into view, a girl, wearing a long white gown which left her arms bare; she carried aloft a burning torch which gave off a great deal of tarry smoke.

'She's supposed to be a virgin,' Zelah explained in a stage whisper, 'but I wouldn't like to bet on that one.'

W.J. Burley lived near Newquay in Cornwall, and was a schoolmaster until he retired to concentrate on his writing. His many Wycliffe books include, most recently, *Wycliffe and the Guild of Nine*. He died in 2002.

By W.J. Burley

WYCLIFFE SERIES
Wycliffe and the Three-Toed Pussy
Wycliffe and How to Kill a Cat
Wycliffe and the Guilt Edged Alibi
Wycliffe and Death in a Salubrious Place
Wycliffe and Death in Stanley Street
Wycliffe and the Pea-Green Boat
Wycliffe and the School Bullies
Wycliffe and the Scapegoat
Wycliffe in Paul's Court
Wycliffe's Wild-Goose Chase
Wycliffe and the Beales
Wycliffe and the Four Jacks
Wycliffe and the Quiet Virgin
Wycliffe and the Winsor Blue
Wycliffe and the Tangled Web
Wycliffe and the Cycle of Death
Wycliffe and the Dead Flautist
Wycliffe and the Last Rites
Wycliffe and the Dunes Mystery
Wycliffe and the House of Fear
Wycliffe and the Redhead
Wycliffe and the Guild of Nine

HENRY PYM SERIES
A Taste of Power
Death in Willow Pattern

OTHER NOVELS
The Schoolmaster
The Sixth Day
Charles and Elizabeth
The House of Care

Wycliffe
AND THE
SCAPEGOAT

W.J. Burley

An Orion paperback

First published in Great Britain in 1978
by Victor Gollancz Ltd
First published in paperback in 1987
by Corgi Books
This paperback edition published in 2003
by Orion Books Ltd,
Orion House, 5 Upper St Martin's Lane,
London WC2H 9EA

An Hachette UK company

3 5 7 9 10 8 6 4

Copyright © W.J. Burley 1978

The right of W.J. Burley to be identified as the
author of this work has been asserted by him in accordance
with the Copyright, Designs and Patents Act 1988.

All rights reserved. No part of this publication may be
reproduced, stored in a retrieval system, or transmitted, in
any form or by any means, electronic, mechanical,
photocopying, recording or otherwise, without the prior
permission of the copyright owner.

A CIP catalogue record for this book is available
from the British Library.

ISBN 978-0-7528-4971-3

Printed and bound in Great Britain by
Clays Ltd, St Ives plc

The Orion Publishing Group's policy is to use papers that
are natural, renewable and recyclable products and
made from wood grown in sustainable forests. The logging
and manufacturing processes are expected to conform to
the environmental regulations of the country of origin.

www.orionbooks.co.uk

WYCLIFFE
AND THE SCAPEGOAT

Chapter One

JONATHAN RIDDLE WALKED down Bethel Street between two rows of identical granite cottages whose front doors opened on to the street. It was a sunny afternoon, warm for October, and some women were gossiping on their doorsteps. They stopped as he passed and he was acutely aware of their collective gaze. 'The undertaker' – that was what they called him, using it as a term of mild contempt. So rarely was he referred to by his name that when people came to see him in his office they often began, 'Mr ...' and had to stop and think before they could remember what he was called. Why did he have to be 'the undertaker'? Why not 'the builder'? or just 'Riddle'? Funerals formed only a small part of his business.

He found it impossible to go about the town in a relaxed and casual way as others seemed to do, for he always felt self-conscious and absurdly vulnerable. Frequently he used his car or one of his vans to go short distances merely to avoid a walk through the streets.

He turned out of Bethel Street into Stockholm Backs and walked briskly to his yard. Double doors, newly painted and tastefully lettered, announced his business: *Jonathan Riddle: Builder, Contractor and Decorator*. An addendum, in smaller letters, read: *Funeral Director*. As he passed through the wicket gate and closed it behind him he experienced an immediate relaxation of tension. It was ridiculous but he felt that he had escaped pursuit.

On his right, a large, open shed housed two trucks, a battery of cement mixers and a new, yellow-painted excavator. In front of him, across the yard, was the workshop, with offices next door. All seemed as it should be; the reassuring whine of the

7

circular saw and the screech of the planing machine drowned all other sounds. As he entered the main office one girl, a little brunette, was on the telephone while another, who had streaks of grey in her hair, was typing.

'Any messages, Miss Hicks?'

The typist turned back a page of her pad. 'Mr Bryant telephoned about our last order.'

'Problems?'

'He said that there might be a delay of up to three weeks on the oak strip.'

'What about the cedar?'

'No difficulty there, he expects to deliver within a week.'

'Is Matthew in?'

'No. He's gone over to Moyle's Farm. Apparently they're having trouble with the foundations for the new implements shed.'

'What sort of trouble?'

'Mr Moyle didn't say; he just asked to speak to Matthew so I put him through.'

'Thank you, Miss Hicks.' He made a point of politeness and formality in dealing with his employees.

He went through to his office and into a cloakroom adjoining. He took off his undertaker's coat with its black satin facings, covered it with a polythene wrap and hung it in a tiny closet. His bowler hat, similarly treated, went on to the shelf above. He moistened a comb and ran it through his hair, sleeking it down, then he studied the result in a mirror over the hand-basin. He turned his head a little to one side then to the other, careful to avoid a near-profile view which would have disclosed the abnormal development of his chin.

He was fifty, and except for a dusting round the temples, his hair was still black, the skin of his lean neck was firm and there were no bags under his eyes nor crow's feet in the corners. He thought that he might pass for five years younger than he was. Laura Passmore, the woman he was going to marry, was thirty-eight. The black coat she had worn that afternoon at her uncle's funeral had set off her blonde hair and fair complexion. She was a very good looking woman and, he thought, a sensible one who

8

would do him credit as his wife. No one nowadays would bother about the fact that she had divorced her husband.

After a lifetime of bachelorhood Riddle had decided to marry for a number of reasons; chief among them was a morbid fear of old age and an irrational belief that he would be the victim of a protracted and demeaning illness when he would need someone who was in duty bound to care for him. He was troubled also by a growing need for companionship, something deeper and more truly intimate than he could achieve with the women he had so far known.

Still eyeing himself in the mirror, he fingered his upper lip. Perhaps a moustache? Broad and well trimmed it might give him a military air and do something to relieve the sallowness of his complexion ...

He heard a movement in the office.

'Is that you, Matthew?'

'Yes, uncle.'

He joined his nephew in the office.

'What's the trouble at Moyle's?'

Like his uncle, Matthew was lean, bony and very dark, but his features were less prominent; in fact he had rather a weak face which, in repose, looked vaguely petulant. He was thirty, the son of Riddle's widowed sister, and he had been with the firm since leaving school. For the past four or five years he had been in virtual charge of the practical side of the business, though liable to be called to account for the smallest decision.

'Fabricon sent us the wrong foundation plans. We set the ragbolts for the stanchions at three metre centres but now our chaps have started to erect it turns out they should have been three metres fifty.'

Riddle's voice was silky. 'Wouldn't it have been wise to check?'

'We put the foundations down before the steel was on the site.'

'Then perhaps we were in too much hurry.'

Spots of colour appeared on Matthew's cheeks. 'But it was you who said that ...'

Riddle's voice acquired an edge. 'Whatever I said or didn't say

9

won't help us now.' He smoothed his great chin. 'What's it going to cost?'

Matthew controlled his indignation. 'Not a great deal; a compressor and a couple of drills with two men for a day – a hundred should cover it.'

Riddle took a tin of white mints from his pocket, opened it and slipped one between his lips.

'A hundred pounds wasted.'

'But we shall be able to claim on Fabricon, it was their –'

'I hope so, indeed. What does Moyle say?'

'He's reasonable, he realises it wasn't our fault.'

'Very understanding of him – but he doesn't have to foot the bill.'

Matthew's irritation broke through. 'But I've told you –'

Riddle waved a large, pale hand. 'Don't get excited, Matthew; you must learn to take criticism. Perhaps you will send in Miss Hicks as you go out, I think she has some letters for me to sign.'

Matthew was useful, but needed to be reminded from time to time who was running the firm. Riddle had hinted once or twice at a junior partnership but he had made no promise.

Miss Hicks came in with the letters and Riddle read every one before adding his signature. He was proud of that signature. The J and the R formed a monogram surrounded by a complex arabesque; the '—iddle' seemed to have been added as an afterthought.

The noise of machinery from the workshop ceased abruptly, leaving a silence which came as a slight shock. Although there was a clock on the wall Riddle took out a silver watch from his waistcoat pocket.

'Half-past five already! The undertaking side of this business takes up a lot of time, Miss Hicks. I sometimes wonder if it's worth it.'

'It's a public service, Mr Riddle.'

He nodded. 'That's true, Miss Hicks, very true.'

Riddle lived in a large stone-built house with an acre of grounds. In his boyhood the house had belonged to a retired general, an autocratic gentleman who employed four or five servants. When the general died the house had remained untenanted for a long time until Riddle bought it. Now, for almost fifteen years, he had lived there with his mother, his widowed sister and her son, Matthew.

'Oh, there you are!'

His sister Sarah, seven years older than he, was tall, heavily built, with large features, a definite moustache and a masculine voice.

He hung his mackintosh in a cloakroom off the hall and changed his shoes for a pair of patent leather slippers. The house had been built in 1890 in neo-Gothic style reminiscent of Pugin and the hall looked like a church porch.

'Your tea will be ready in ten minutes.'

Riddle did not answer; they exchanged very little small talk. He crossed the hall and entered the drawing-room, which had a large bay window looking out on the gravelled drive. The furniture, which included a lot of red plush, had come with the house; so had the grand piano which none of them could play. Sarah followed him in.

'Sidney Passmore phoned.' Sidney was the brother of Laura's ex-husband.

'What did he want?' he asked mechanically though he knew well enough.

'He didn't say. He's coming over this evening.' She lingered. 'Surely you must have seen him at the funeral?'

'You can't talk business at a funeral.'

Sarah never tired of prying, though he told her very little – just enough to whet her appetite for more. It was a game they played, but a game in which there was very little goodwill.

'I told him you would be in – you will, won't you?'

'Yes.'

When he married he would have to make provision for his mother and Sarah. Obligations: they grew on a man like hair. He had no liking for Sarah – over the years she had become slovenly in her person and habits so that she often repelled him – but she was his sister.

Laura Passmore. The image of her as he had seen her that afternoon kept returning to his mind. He had given a great deal

11

of thought to the subject of marriage and long before her divorce was even in prospect he had admired her and hoped that he might find a woman of her age and stamp. He had toyed with the idea of marrying a young girl; one often read of men of his age or older marrying young girls of eighteen or nineteen, and all his erotic fancies concerned such girls, but he had the sense to see that a young woman would marry him only for his money while an older woman would value the security he could offer, a very different matter. There would be a contract, the terms of which would be clearly understood, mutually though tacitly agreed.

And there was Hilda, Laura's sixteen-year-old daughter. What would it be like to be her step-father? Living in the same house was bound to entail some intimacy. He had a vivid and shameful vision which he banished from his mind. And three-year-old Harold: his attitude to the little boy puzzled him by its ambivalence. The child was bound to be a liability, a tie, making demands on Laura which would conflict with and no doubt take precedence over her obligations to him. Against that he would bring up the boy as his own, a ready-made son. He had made up his mind that there would be no children of the marriage, for the business of pregnancy and birth revolted him. Moreover there was something in his nature, perhaps a hidden flaw in his self conceit, which made him dread parenthood.

He heard Matthew come in and go up to his room.

It was a pity that the business with Sidney should crop up now, though he did not think that Laura had any regard for her ex-husband's family.

'Your tea's ready.'

The dining-room was at the back of the house, a gloomy room looking out through french windows to a thicket of laurels. The oval table was laid for four. Cold ham and tongue, some limp lettuce and a few tomatoes; there was a plate of bread and butter and a fruit cake which, like all Sarah's cakes, would be soggy in the middle. His mother was already in her place and he went over to put his lips to her forehead.

'Hullo, mother.'

She was still an impressive figure, with strong, angular features and surprisingly youthful brown eyes. Her white hair was gathered into a tight bun at the back and she wore a magenta cardigan over a high-necked, grey silk blouse.

'Was it a good funeral?'

'Very good, mother. A lot of people and everything went without a hitch.'

The old lady helped herself generously to cold meat and took a slice of bread and butter.

'This bread is dry, Sarah, like sawdust. Left over from yesterday, I'll bet!' she muttered disagreeably before turning again to her son. 'I suppose Laura Passmore was there?'

'Naturally; she was his niece.' He and Laura had not yet told anyone of their intention to marry but he suspected that his mother and Sarah had somehow informed themselves.

Sarah said: 'I see in the paper that her divorce has come through.' When Riddle said nothing, she went on: 'But it won't be long before she gets her hooks in another man.'

'Pass me the mayonnaise, Sarah, please.' Riddle's manner was peremptory. He took the jar she passed to him; it was sticky on the outside.

Sometimes he imagined coming home to meals that were well prepared and tastefully served; meals to be eaten in a bright room off sparkling china on a white cloth. There would be flowers and his companion would be clean, crisp and comely . . .

The fretted overmantel was dusty, the little inset mirrors had a bluish bloom, the curtains and carpets looked faded and tired. Sarah had a woman in every day but the rooms were never properly cleaned.

'She thought she'd got rid of that husband of hers but he's back.' The old lady was not easily intimidated. 'Ernie's living in one of the caravans on his brother's site.'

Matthew came in and sat in his place with a muttered word. He helped himself to ham and lettuce.

'There's a tomato, Matthew.'

'You know I never touch tomato, mother.'

His grandmother looked at him with disapproval. 'You should. No wonder you get boils.'

It was true that Matthew had suffered a succession of boils in recent months.

'You've fixed up for the compressor to be at Moyle's in the morning?'

'Yes, uncle.'

Riddle's gaze rested on his nephew; Matthew met his eyes for a moment then looked down at his plate.

This business with Sidney Passmore was a complication. Although Laura's ex-husband, Ernie, had specialised in living off social security, his brother, Sidney, was prosperous. He and his wife ran a large boarding house and he had the only camping and caravan site within easy reach of the town. Five years ago he had bought a field and put caravans on it; now he rented four adjoining fields. The site had proper sanitation, hot showers, a shop and a cafeteria. It was these rented fields which were the cause of the present trouble.

Riddle sighed.

The silence in the dining-room was complete. Sometimes when the four of them were sitting down to a meal he would listen to the silence for minutes together. It seemed to grow, to become palpable, almost menacing until he could stand it no longer and was forced to speak. He was convinced that they did it on purpose, for these silences usually followed an occasion when, as now, he had cut short a line of talk of which he disapproved.

Not one of them would meet his eyes, not even his mother.

'Are you going out this evening, Sarah?'

Sarah put her hand to her mouth to cover a belch. 'There's a W.I. meeting, but I could stay in until Sidney comes.'

'Don't put yourself out on my account.' He turned to his nephew. 'What about you, Matthew?'

Matthew looked up from his plate as though startled at being addressed.

'Me? Yes, I shall probably go out for a while.'

Sarah said, 'If you've finished I'll clear away.'

He went up to the first floor room which he called his study. As he climbed the oak staircase, past the tall, stained-glass window, he was seeing the house with new eyes. It had been a mistake. Who was impressed? They sneered behind his back. 'The undertaker trying to pretend ...'

His room was in the front of the house and looked out over

14

the sea. A flat topped desk stood by the window; there was a swivel-chair upholstered in worn, black leather. Bookshelves against two of the walls were full of books with faded spines – works on building construction, law and accountancy – and there were hundreds of unbound technical journals dating back more than twenty years. An electric fire stood in the fireplace and on the wall above it there was a large-scale map of the town and district.

He closed the door behind him and stood for a moment, overcome by a feeling of intense depression.

Sidney Passmore arrived just before eight o'clock. He was flushed, his sparse, sandy hair was dishevelled, and Riddle guessed that he had spent some time in the pub priming himself with Dutch courage. Little beads of perspiration stood out on his freckled forehead and he was excited though doing his best to appear calm. His wife, Elsie, would have briefed him for Sidney was no businessman.

'I wanted to see you –'

'Have a seat, Sidney.' Riddle brought up a chair to the desk.

'I was going –'

'You look warm.'

Sidney perched himself on the edge of his chair, knees apart, hands on his knees. His manner and posture were aggressive but his heart was not in it.

'I reckon you don't need to be told why I've come.'

'About the fields?'

Sidney gestured angrily. 'What's your game? That's what I want to know.'

Riddle took one of his little white mints and put it in his mouth. 'No game, Sidney. The fields were for sale and I bought them.'

'That's a bloody lie for a start! That land was never on the market.'

'If Mrs Trewin had been unwilling to sell, how could I have bought it?'

'You badgered the old lady. Joe scarcely cold in his grave and you sniffing round his widow to see what you could pick up.'

Riddle studied his long, white fingers. 'Joe Trewin has been

15

dead for four months. As you know, the old lady has been staying with her daughter in Plymouth. I happened to be in Plymouth and I called. I asked her if she wanted to sell and she said that she did, it was as simple as that. You had the same opportunity.'

Sidney blustered. 'I was waiting until she came back like any decent man would. In any case, I had an arrangement with Joe; he didn't want to sell in his lifetime but he told me that I should have first option when he was gone ...'

'Whatever arrangement he made with you, he evidently didn't tell his wife about it. You should have got something in writing, Sidney.'

The flush on Sidney's face deepened. 'You're a bastard, Riddle. I know why you want my land – you think it'll go for building and you stand to make a packet, but you want to watch out for the new Act.'

Riddle said nothing. He was staring out of the window; the dingy, dusty little room was flooded with golden light from the setting sun.

Sidney passed his hand over his forehead; he was not an aggressive man and despite his indignation he was well aware of the weakness of his position.

'Without that land my site is finished.'

'You still have your original field.'

'Damn near covered with buildings – toilets, showers, shop, cafe, camp-shelter – there's hardly room left for three lousy tents. I'm dependent on those fields and you know it. If it's a question of money I'll give you a fair return on the deal ...'

There was a faint smile on Riddle's lips. He was thinking: 'He blusters but he's soft inside.' He watched the sun set. The sky was cloudless and the great orange ball just dipped into the sea. It was over quite quickly; a brilliant, thin segment seemed to linger, then it vanished. Almost at once the blue-green sky began to fade.

To him it was incredible that anyone could invest thousands of pounds in a venture involving land over which he had no vestige of legal control, just the word of an ailing old man.

'Would you consider an offer?' Sidney was almost pleading.
'I didn't buy to sell again.'

'A lease then – ten years. We could come to terms, I'm sure.'

Riddle was thinking: 'Because he's popular and he's got a bit of capital, he thinks he can run a business. But there's more to it than that. You have to keep one jump ahead and then it doesn't matter whether they like you or whether they don't.'

'I had a letter from your solicitor yesterday and I haven't slept since.' Sidney's large, freckled hands were clasped together; all signs of anger had disappeared. 'Whatever the planners decide it won't be for four or five years, you'll have no use for the land until – '

'I'll make *you* an offer, Sidney.'

'An offer?' Sidney clutched at hope as a drowning man grabs a life-raft. 'What sort of offer?'

'For your field and the buildings on it.'

It took a moment for the proposal to sink in, then Sidney looked at him in ludicrous astonishment. 'You must be mad!'

'Think it over.'

'There's nothing to think over. I'll see you in hell before I hand you my living on a bloody plate.'

'Then there's no more to be said.'

Sidney stood up. 'We'll see about that.' He stood foolishly for a moment, not knowing what to do or say, then he turned on his heel and let himself out. Riddle heard him on the stairs, then the front door banged.

At half-past ten Sarah made cocoa and brought it into the drawing-room where Riddle was reading. Two mugs of cocoa and some rich tea biscuits. Their mother had already gone to bed.

Sarah sat on the edge of a wing-back chair. Her manner was habitually aggressive but with her brother she was careful not to go too far.

'What's the matter with you?'

Riddle did not answer directly. 'Is Matthew in?'

'Not yet.'

'He's late.'

'He's old enough to please himself.'

17

Riddle nibbled a biscuit. 'He's got something on his mind, he's been edgy for months. Do you think it's a girl?'

'I shouldn't be surprised. It's time he was married anyway, he's thirty.'

Riddle said nothing, sensing what would come next.

'I thought you were going to do something for the boy, give him some encouragement ...'

'We'll see.'

Sarah made a disdainful noise. Riddle sipped his cocoa and changed the subject.

'Do you remember Sidney Passmore when he was at school with me?'

Her wary eyes sought his. 'Of course I remember him, why?'

Riddle smiled. 'Sidney and his brother Ernie, all the girls were after that pair.'

'Not surprising, they were good looking lads.'

'I used to envy them.'

Sarah looked at him, trying to make up her mind where this was leading.

'Now Ernie lives off social security and his wife has divorced him. And Sidney is ...'

'Sidney is what?'

Riddle made a vague gesture and his sister looked at him, puzzled. 'What's got into you tonight?'

Riddle sat at his desk. Rain drummed on the flat roof of the offices and almost drowned the noise of the machinery in the workshops. A small tic affected the right-hand corner of the undertaker's mouth, a sure sign that he was either upset or pleasurably excited – it was impossible to judge which. It was a week after his interview with Sidney.

He picked up the telephone. 'Is Matthew there?'

'No, Mr Riddle ... Just a minute, I think he's now crossing the yard.'

'Ask him to come in, please.'

Riddle arranged the papers on his desk into three piles – advice notes, delivery notes and invoices – then he sat, drumming his fingers on the desk until Matthew came in. He had

18

taken off his oilskins but his hair was wet and little globules of water trickled down his forehead.

'You wanted me, uncle?'

'Yes, Matthew. Sit down, please.'

The young man looked ill, his natural pallor accentuated by hollow cheeks and a darkness round the eyes.

'You don't look well, Matthew.'

Matthew forced animation into his voice. 'I'm all right, uncle, I didn't sleep very well last night, that's all.'

Riddle looked at his nephew and Matthew studied the top of the desk.

'Perhaps you've got something on your mind?'

Matthew's lips were trembling and his attempt to sound cheerfully off-hand was betrayed by a break in his voice. 'No, uncle, not a thing.'

'Then you should have,' Riddle snapped. 'You know what these are?' He held up the invoices.

'Invoices from Bryant, the builders' merchants.'

'And these?'

Riddle held up in turn the advice notes and delivery notes for Matthew to identify. The voice in which he did so was scarcely audible.

'And it's your job to check deliveries against the notes and the notes against the invoices – is that right?'

The young man nodded, unable to speak.

Riddle made a parade of going through the papers and comparing them. 'All the items listed here have been ticked off on the three sets of documents. As they refer to the same deliveries on August 14th, September 5th, and September 21st, they should correspond – that is so, isn't it?'

Matthew nodded once more.

Riddle frowned. 'But they do not correspond; there are discrepancies – substantial discrepancies. For example, on the invoice for goods delivered on August 14th we are charged for a W.C. suite in green and a stainless-steel sink-top, neither of which appear on the corresponding delivery note. On this invoice for goods delivered on — '

'I'm sorry, uncle, I must have made a mistake.'

19

Riddle shuffled the papers together and pushed them to one side. He sat back in his chair, the fingertips of his hands meeting.

'How long has this been going on, Matthew?'

'I don't know what you mean.'

'You know perfectly well what I mean and it is useless for you to lie. I spent a good part of last weekend with Mr Bryant at his office. We uncovered a nasty little conspiracy between you and one of his despatch clerks, a certain Alfred Weekes. The goods invoiced to me and not despatched were sold to jobbing builders at cut prices and the proceeds were shared between the two of you. Weekes has been sacked, the question now is what I am to do with you.'

Matthew sat motionless, staring at the desk, and said nothing.

'I asked you how long this has been going on and I want an answer.'

'For about six months.'

Riddle nodded. 'That, at least, agrees with the information we got from Weekes.'

'I'll pay you back, uncle, every penny.'

'Oh, yes, Matthew, you'll pay me back. The sum involved is in the neighbourhood of eight hundred pounds. Presumably you shared equally with Weekes, but as he has lost his job there is little prospect of getting anything from him.'

Matthew looked up for the first time. 'You mean that I shall have to pay it all back?'

'Of course! What else do you expect? You are very lucky indeed to escape prosecution. If you had not been my nephew that is what would have happened to you and your accomplice.'

'You'll deduct so much a month from my salary?'

Riddle looked at the sallow, weak face but his expression was blank. 'No, Matthew, that would be too easy. On the first of each month I shall expect to receive your cheque for forty pounds, which means that your debt will be discharged in twenty months from now. You will notice that I am making no interest charge, but if you fail to make any payment promptly you will be dismissed from your post with the firm.'

'Forty pounds, uncle! I doubt if I can ...'

Riddle gestured impatiently. 'It's up to you, Matthew, it's your choice. That's all I have to say except that to all outward appearance both here and at home things must continue as before. You understand?'

'Yes, uncle.' Matthew stood up to go.

'Nothing to be said to your mother.'

'No.'

'One more thing; where did the money go?'

Matthew stood by the desk, looking vague. 'Where did it go?'

'That is what I asked you. You have your salary, you are unmarried and you live in my house making only a nominal contribution for your board and lodging; it seems reasonable to ask why you needed this money.'

Matthew shook his head.

'Are you gambling?'

'No, uncle.'

'Is it women?'

Another shake of the head.

Riddle shrugged. 'Very well, it's your affair, not mine. But make no mistake, if there is any further irregularity you will not get off because you are my nephew.'

It was Friday, the last Friday of the month; Riddle went round his workshop with a wooden tray bearing the wages envelopes of his men. He handed each man his wages and got him to sign against his name in a little black book. Afterwards he took his car and drove to the various sites where his men were working and repeated the routine. Matthew went with him to answer queries about the progress of the work. This Friday ritual was the high point of the undertaker's week.

'Here you are, Jim, I've brought your money.'

'Thank you, Mr Riddle.'

'Try not to spend it all at once.'

Or:

'I was sorry to hear about Joyce, is she out of hospital yet?'

'Coming out tomorrow.'

'Good! Wish her well for me.'

He was the source of their security; it was his enterprise which enabled them to earn their livings. There were a few militants who would have resented what they would see as patronage, but he knew who they were and handed them their money in silence.

Back to the office to sign his correspondence then home to tea.

Now that the evenings were closing in the curtains were drawn over the french windows when they had tea. The electric light filtering through a discoloured shade had a greenish tinge which made the food look even less appetising and the room more depressing.

He gave his mother the ritual kiss and took his place at the table.

'Matthew isn't home yet.' Sarah passed him a segment of cheese flan.

'No, he's gone to see a client about an estimate. He told me he probably wouldn't be home for a meal but would go on wherever it was he was going for the evening.'

'And where was that?'

'I didn't ask him.'

'You expect too much of that boy, Jonathan.'

'Matthew is not a boy, Sarah; when I was his age I was running my own business.'

'Yes, and you were getting a sight more out of it than he is.'

Riddle's lips twitched. 'Exactly, it was *my* business.'

The old lady made a noise with her lips, an explosive sound. 'Boy's a milksop. No guts.'

The inevitable silence enveloped them and lengthened, but today there was something Riddle wanted to say. Several times he cleared his throat and formed his lips but did not speak. It was absurd the way tension was building up inside him; he thought he could feel little beads of perspiration on his forehead, though the room was clammily cold.

The old lady poured milk into her cup and reached for the teapot. All she got from it was a thin trickle.

Sarah said, 'Give it here, I'll make some more.'

'Not for me.' She drew her shawl round her. 'I think I'll go upstairs, this room is like a tomb.'

'Just a minute, mother . . .' He had started to speak but could not find the words to go on.

His mother looked at him. 'Well?'

He swallowed hard. 'There's something I wanted to say to you and to Sarah.'

The two women sat immobile, faces expressionless.

'I've decided to get married.'

Sarah sniffed. 'So it's true!'

'And who is it you're going to marry?' The old woman was looking at him with an expression in which amusement was blended with contempt.

'Laura Passmore.'

His mother raised her hands in a gesture of pretended incredulity. 'You must be soft in the head, Jonathan!'

Sarah fixed her shrewd eyes on him. 'Are you thinking of bringing her here?'

He smoothed the tablecloth with his huge hand. 'No, that's another thing, I intend to put this house on the market or to convert it into flats.'

'Oh? And what happens to us – to mother and me? After all these years . . .'

'I'm willing to buy a smaller place, easier to run, just for mother and you, Sarah. When I'm married I shall be living in one of the houses I'm building on Beacon Hill.'

'For Laura Passmore? You'll have to watch it or she'll be keeping the coal in the bath.'

Sarah realised that she had gone too far but there was nothing she could do about it. Her brother looked at her with hard, cold eyes. 'Well, Sarah, that's how it's going to be. You can take my offer of a smaller house for you and mother or you can get out and fend for yourself.'

'And if I go, what happens to mother?'

'Mother won't suffer, she would come to live with me.'

The old woman became truly indignant for the first time. 'Me live with that woman? I'd rather go into an institution!'

Riddle stood up, looked for a moment at the pair of them and said, quietly: 'Then you'll have to sort something out between you, won't you? I'm going to the yard this evening.'

They heard him go upstairs to his room.

A few minutes later Matthew came in. 'I'm going to a film in Penzance, I shall be back between eleven and half-past.'

And still the two women sat on in silence. They heard Riddle come downstairs, change his shoes in the closet, then the front door slammed.

'You and I will have to have a talk, mother,' Sarah said.

Riddle walked down the hill from his house then turned off along one of the terraces. A fine mist blew in from the sea and the lights of the town below were visible as a vague glow. His heart was racing but he felt a certain exhilaration, for he had done what he most dreaded doing. He had never before had a real confrontation with either his mother or his sister and he had doubted his ability to handle one when it came.

Really it had been much easier than he had feared. He thought that they had accepted the situation; there would be sulks but no overt protests – no *rows*. He hated rows.

He had said that he was going to the yard and he often did return to work there in the evenings but not on Fridays. He avoided the town, following a route which took him round the outskirts, losing height all the way.

'Goodnight, Mr Riddle.'

There was just enough light from a street lamp for him to recognise the young girl from the office, cuddled up to a youth with long, lank fair hair. He heard them giggle after he had passed and the boy called after him, mimicking the girl, 'Goodnight, Mr Riddle.'

A very steep hill with a hairpin bend at the bottom brought him to a narrow road which ran by the sea on the western outskirts of the town.

He had another confrontation ahead of him if he was to embark on marriage with the slate wiped clean.

He turned toward the town; on his right the ground sloped up steeply, so steeply that it had never been built over; on his left there was a very low cliff, a tumble of rocks and the sea. At one

24

point a solitary house had been built out on a platform. It was small, surrounded by wooden palings and had steps going up to the front door. Although it was dark and the road twisted away in both directions he stood still and listened for several seconds before going up the steps and ringing the bell. A subdued glow through the curtains of a window on the left of the door was the only sign of life. He had to wait a little while before his ring was answered.

'You're early tonight.'

He was admitted to a tiny hall lit by a heavily shaded ceiling lamp. She took his coat, shook it briefly and hung it in the hall cupboard. He followed her into a cosy sitting-room with a window at each end. There was an open fire, a long settee and two easy chairs. A colour television was showing a comedy programme with frequent exaggerated bursts of laughter from the invisible audience. She switched it off.

She was still young with attractive features but substantially overweight. She had a mop of very dark hair and she wore a floral housecoat with the lacy top of an underslip showing at the neck. Her legs were bare and she wore furry slippers. Without a word she went to a side table, where there were drinks and a little dish of nuts and raisins. She poured two glasses of sherry and brought them to the settee.

'Anything wrong?'

He shook his head. 'No, why?'

'You seem preoccupied.'

'Not more than usual.'

She laughed, a rich, gurgling sound. Like most fat girls she had a pleasant voice.

'The poor man is overworked.'

She handed him his sherry and ran her plump fingers through his carefully plastered hair. He twisted his head away.

In the silence he could hear the sea washing over the rocks. He had been there when the noise was deafening and torrents of spray beat against the window from each wave.

'Mary ...'

'Yes, Johnny?'

'Nothing.'

25

She sipped her sherry and watched him. Everything about her was warm and of a fleshy softness. He finished his drink and put the glass on the floor.

'Why are they all against me, Mary?'

She took his hand. 'They're jealous, Johnny, that's all it is.'

'Jealous? I wish I could believe that.'

She guided his hand inside her slip. 'Anyway, Johnny, I'm not against you, am I?'

'Even young Matthew ... You'd think that he ...'

'What about Matthew, Johnny? What's he been doing?' She was undoing his shirt buttons.

'Nothing. Nothing of any importance.'

Chapter Two

THE HEADLAND SLOPED in a hollow curve to the sea and at its very crest, raised on an inclined plane like the launching ramp of a ship, was the Wheel. It stood within a ring of hissing pressure lamps which kept the darkness at bay. An elaborate framework of twisted osiers, the Wheel was nine feet in diameter with the proportions of a water-wheel; but lit by the lamps and raised aloft as it was, it looked gigantic. The osiers were almost hidden by plaited straw and by interlacing branches of yew and laurel; coloured streamers attached to the rim hung limply on the still air and within the Wheel, in a bower of straw and foliage, was a life-size figure wearing a grotesque mask and enveloped in a black cloak. Here was the embodiment of evil, the Scapegoat, and with his imminent destruction wickedness would be symbolically cast out and the townspeople would be once more on the side of the angels.

They were out in strength, a milling crowd, grouping and regrouping, like ants disturbed. Children who bravely ventured into the darkness soon came scampering back. It was October 31st, All-Hallows Eve, and only credit balances in several hundred bank accounts recalled summer visitors who had swarmed over the streets and beaches and cliffs between June and September. The town had settled to being itself again, sleepy, clannish, introverted. In a little while the Wheel would be set alight, released from its cradle and allowed to trundle down the slope, gathering momentum. Thunder flashes, Roman candles and other pyrotechnics would enliven its passage until, a spinning hoop of flame, it launched itself over the cliff, described a brief trajectory and plunged into the sea, never to be seen again.

27

At least, that was the theory. Most years it was washed up again on the next or a later tide, but this was of no consequence so long as the Scapegoat had gone. More seriously, on one or two occasions, the Wheel had not reached the sea but had left its appointed path to run amok in the gorse and heather, starting fires. Such mishaps were bad omens, and though the townspeople maintained that they did not take the Wheel seriously they were happier when all went according to plan.

For days before Hallowe'en several men devoted their spare time to preparing the track; the grass was trimmed, weeds and stones removed, hollows and gullies washed out by the rain were filled and the whole course was meticulously surveyed for snags and bumps. The custodianship of the path had become the prerogative of a few specialists with a fund of empirical knowledge which they gravely applied to securing the smooth passage of the Wheel. Now, for safety, the path was roped off on either side.

Detective Chief Superintendent Wycliffe and his wife, Helen, were to see the spectacle for the first time; they were spending a long weekend with the Ballards, who lived on the moor above the town. Tony Ballard was a painter and his wife, Zelah, wrote historical novels. Tony, shy and introverted, lived for his painting, while Zelah seemed to live as she wrote, with an engaging panache.

It was a mild night with clouds drifting across the sky and occasionally obscuring the new moon. Out to sea the beam of the lighthouse swept a great arc every fifteen seconds; on one side of the headland were the lights of the town and harbour, on the other it was just possible to make out a line of cliffs receding into the darkness.

Wycliffe was content; with his hands thrust deep into the pockets of his mackintosh, he watched the crowd, an occupation of which he never tired. People are so much more varied and interesting than birds or badgers or any of the other creatures naturalists watch with such exemplary patience. But Wycliffe's interest was far from scientific; he reached no profound sociological conclusions; he did not even attempt to

28

be objective. On the contrary, he was satisfied to feel that he was sharing in other people's lives.

Teenaged boys paraded in groups of three or four, jostling each other, laughing and shouting; groups of girls, on the whole less brash and aggressive, giggled and chattered, calling to the boys whenever they were in range. Young couples strolled with their arms round each other, pausing now and then to kiss; older couples stopped to greet friends and while the women talked their husbands stood by looking foolishly amiable.

A disembodied voice came over the amplifiers instructing people to move outside the ropes.

'Let's find a good place, Tony, where we can see.'

Opinion was divided over the best place to stand, for if they watched the launching they missed a close-up view of the final plunge into the sea. Zelah favoured the launching site, so that was where they stood.

'We can take a good look at the Wheel,' she explained with embarrassing stridency. 'Of course, originally, it was no effigy tied up in there, but a live man, a human scapegoat. Later, when people got squeamish about that sort of thing, they substituted cats – a dozen or so live cats tied up in a sack. Not that they had anything against cats as cats, but witches were believed to take the form of cats, so it was all quite reasonable, really.'

Zelah seemed to know everybody and the Wycliffes were introduced to a bewildering variety of people whom they never expected to see again.

An eerie blast on a horn signalled the start of the ceremony and the crowd became silent. The master of ceremonies, in a white, druidical robe, mounted the platform by the launching ramp and stood, peering inland along another path, marked off by ropes which disappeared into the darkness. After a while a flickering light appeared in the distance and drew steadily nearer; a torch-bearer came into view, a girl, wearing a long white gown which left her arms bare; she carried aloft a burning torch which gave off a great deal of tarry smoke.

'She's supposed to be a virgin,' Zelah explained in a stage whisper, 'but I wouldn't like to bet on that one.'

The girl mounted the steps to stand beside the master of

ceremonies and they carried on a conversation which, though audible, was unintelligible.

'They're speaking in Cornish,' Zelah said. 'He's asking her if she has brought the need-fire and she tells him that she has. He says: "Was this flame kindled at the altar of the Lord?" and she answers: "This flame was kindled at the holy fire." Actually she lights her torch at one of the candles in the church and somebody runs her up here in a car while she holds the torch out of the window. Of course, that's not how it's supposed to be done.'

The white-robed man took the torch from the girl and held it up to the people. He said a few words which Zelah translated as: 'This is the holy flame which shall consume our wickedness and purge our people of evil for the year to come.'

A few people shouted the proper response, which sounded like, 'Sans! Sans!' Zelah said that it meant, 'Holy! Holy!'

After that the torch was applied to a point on the Wheel and at the same moment the chocks were knocked away. The Wheel seemed to hesitate, then it began to roll very slowly. Flames licked over the straw, which crackled and flared, and the Wheel was clear of the ramp and bowling gently down the cleared path. The first fireworks exploded and the Wheel was almost enveloped in flame while the air was filled with a mixture of smells – paraffin, sooty smoke from the straw and cordite from the fireworks. The Scapegoat appeared unharmed and was clearly visible through the curtain of fire, turning over and over as the Wheel rolled. It began to pick up speed and as it did so larger fireworks were detonated, so that showers of sparks and clouds of coloured smoke trailed behind like a peacock's tail, green and red and blue.

Faster and faster the Wheel trundled, a whirling fiery hoop, until it reached an artificial mound at the cliff edge and was deflected up into the air. It sailed in a great arc, hung poised for a fraction of a second, then plunged out of sight to the sea. Even from where the Wycliffes stood the effect was spectacular. Within seconds of the Wheel disappearing from sight the red glow was extinguished.

A spontaneous cry arose from the crowd followed by a moment of silence, then people began to talk again.

'A good show this year; not a hitch.'

After the ceremony of the Wheel there was a firework display and people bought chips and hot-dogs from traders with vans who were cashing in on the occasion.

The sky, which had been clear and filled with stars, was clouding over and a moist wind blew in from the sea.

'This smells like rain,' Zelah said. 'We don't want to be caught up in the rush when it comes.' She rounded up her charges before the others began to move and willed them along the path to the car park.

Wycliffe and Tony would have preferred to linger, to digest the experience, but they had no choice. They found the Ballards' car.

'Will you drive, Tony, or shall I?'

'You drive, dear.'

Wycliffe and Tony got into the back; Helen was in front with Zelah. In no time at all they were coasting down the slope out of the car park.

'What did you think of it?'

'Very impressive.'

'Oh, it was really worth seeing.'

'Good! You must come again next year and see it from the cliff edge.' Zelah really meant what she said; she was perfectly sincere in making an arrangement for twelve months ahead, never considering the possibilities of change.

They reached the town and drove through its narrow, deserted streets, then they began the long, steady climb to the moor.

'Tony did some sketches last year and he was going to work them up into a picture – why haven't you, Tony?'

The Ballard house was built into the side of a hill, a long, low granite building which had once been something to do with a mine. Huge boulders littered their garden and gorse and heather encroached wherever they were permitted to survive. The house was reached by a stony drive more than half-a-mile long, furrowed and rutted by the drainage from the hill, but they had electricity, oil-fired central heating and no neighbours.

The living-room was long and low with roof-beams which still bore marks of the adze; the fireplace, built of rough-hewn stone, was phoney but acceptable and the walls were white. Tony's Cornish landscapes, in frames of plain gilt, looked well; their rich browns, yellows and orange tones warmed the room and more than balanced the white walls. There were bookcases of dark oak and a solitary shelf for Zelah's own books; nine titles in different editions with a sprinkling of foreign imprints. There was an expanse of untenanted shelf, presumably to allow for future production.

'Whisky, Charles?' Tony poured drinks.

The two men were about the same age, nearing fifty; both were of the lean kind with strong features and over-thin lips; both were taciturn and found it difficult to put ideas into words. Of all the friends with whom Helen had involved him, Wycliffe felt most at ease with Tony. Zelah was a cross to be borne more or less cheerfully and Helen could handle her, when necessary, by being devastatingly blunt. On such occasions Zelah would shrug and say, 'Oh, well, if that's how you want it, my child!' At heart she was a kindly woman.

Zelah was older than her husband; she had straight, short, grey hair and a small, thin face which was never in repose. She did everything with quick, darting movements in which violence was barely restrained. When she used her typewriter she seemed intent on hammering holes in the paper.

Wycliffe was never at ease in other people's houses and not only because he was usually bored. He had never discovered when it was proper to follow his host about and when it was politic to be elsewhere. Now he sat by the fire with his whisky, a drink he did not care for, making conversation with Tony and hoping that it would soon be time for bed. Zelah was telling Helen the plot of her next novel.

'How long have these fire festivals been going on?'

Tony took his time; his responses were always sluggish. 'According to the town guide they date back to Celtic times. I expect you know that November 1st is supposed to have been the start of the Celtic year. They were allowed to lapse in the late nineteenth century and were not revived until after the last war. The chap you saw in the druid outfit got them going again and he's still the king-pin.'

Tony sipped his whisky and stirred the fire before going on: 'He's a strange chap; he runs a small-holding on the moor not far from here. His name is Jordan. He says that his ancestors came over here from Brittany in the seventeenth century, fleeing from Catholic persecution.' Tony smoothed his hand over his thinning hair. 'I think he's probably a bit mixed up in matters of doctrine but he claims to be a "true protestant" not, as he says, a Lutheran protestant. His protest, apparently, goes back a lot further, to the Synod of Whitby when, according to him, the Celtic Christian Church was sold down the river to Rome.'

Wycliffe knocked out his pipe in the grate. 'But surely, that show tonight can't have much to do with Christianity, Celtic or otherwise?'

Tony smiled. 'The vicar would certainly agree with you, but you should talk to Jordan, though not unless you have half a day to spare.'

'His daughter, Cissie, has just had an illegitimate baby,' Zelah chimed in. However deeply involved she might be in her own conversation she rarely missed anything that was said by those around her. 'I listen with my writer's ear,' she would say.

'It's our great local mystery at the moment; nobody knows who the father is except, perhaps, Cissie, and if she knows she's not telling.'

Next day, Sunday – All Saints' Day – Wycliffe woke at seven, but it was after eight before he dared get out of bed and peer through the curtains, for Helen was still asleep. Their bedroom was in the front of the house and looked out over the sea, a vast expanse of blue, sparkling in early morning sunshine. At first it looked empty, then he saw two small vessels, just short of the horizon, their motion imperceptible. Away to his right the lighthouse stood on its rocky island like a picture in a story book and it all reminded him of his first holiday by the sea at the age of seven. He wondered if he might take a walk before the others were up. He washed and dressed quietly and stole into the kitchen, only to find Zelah making coffee. She grinned at him.

'I heard you moving about. Here, help yourself . . .'

She was wearing a dressing gown with a pattern of Chinese dragons.

'Bored?'

'Of course not!'

'Liar!'

At half-past eleven he went down to the town with Tony to collect the papers.

'Lunch at one, sharp!' Zelah called after them. 'This afternoon we are going over to Trengirth Hill.'

When they had collected the papers from a shop on the wharf Tony took him to *The Brigantine*, a pub halfway up a steep, cobbled street. A notice at the bottom of the street warned that it was unsuitable for motors. The bar had not been tarted up, it had a stone floor, chocolate-painted woodwork and buff walls which were hung with oleographs of old sailing vessels. There were a fair number of customers and Tony was greeted by several.

'You must try their special, Charles, it's from a private brewery.'

Wycliffe was surprised to see the shy Tony on such good terms with the company. They took their drinks and sat next to a lean, gaunt individual with a twisted lip, whom Tony addressed as Titch. When they had been seated for some time Titch said: 'I suppose you've heard the news?'

'What news?'

'The undertaker is missing.'

'Riddle?'

Titch did not bother to answer.

'How long since?'

'Friday evening. He went out at half-seven and told Sarah he was going to the yard to work on the books.' Titch took a gulp of beer and wiped his mouth on his sleeve. 'Nobody's seen him since.'

Like the good storyteller he was, Titch allowed time for this to sink in before going on. 'Sarah didn't know he wasn't home until she went to call him next morning and found he hadn't slept in his bed. Matthew was sent off to the yard, but Riddle wasn't there and Matthew reckoned he hadn't been there.'

Another pause.

'They've called in the police. Sarah was down at the nick this morning.'

'Did he take his car?'

'No. From what I've heard he didn't take his car and he didn't take one of his vans either.'

'What do you think has happened to him?'

Titch took time to consider the question. 'There's all sorts of rumours, but you can't take notice of rumours in this place. If he doesn't turn up at his yard in the morning I'll believe something's really happened to him. Either he'll be dead or he'll have found some place where he can make money quicker.'

There was a general laugh at this and the subject was dropped.

By Monday evening the Wycliffes were back at The Watch House, their home outside the city where he had his headquarters, and on Tuesday morning he was in his office.

November was living up to its reputation. A grey drizzle enveloped the city; where there were trees, sodden leaves choked the drains and made the pavements dangerous. Despite the much vaunted heating and ventilating system of the new police headquarters the windows of Wycliffe's office were almost obscured by condensation and the air had a clammy warmth which reminded him of the tropical house at Kew.

His in-tray was piled high with papers and his clerical assistant, WPC Diane Saxton, stood over him, polite but relentless.

'That's a draft of a proposed new crime prevention leaflet. Mr Bellings would like your comments on it today if possible . . . Oh, yes, that's rather urgent. Detective Constables Rowse and Calder and Detective Sergeant Bourne are up before the next Promotion Board and your reports haven't gone in yet.' She skilfully prevented him from slipping the crime prevention leaflet in at the bottom of the pile.

'The new duty rosters need your approval . . . Accounts want your comments on the expense sheets of several officers engaged on the Throgmorton case . . .'

'Including mine, I expect?'

'Including yours, sir ... And there's another memo from Accounts asking for your views on possible economies in telephone and postal costs ... No, don't miss that one, sir, it's important – the chief wants your ideas for reorganisation and co-ordination of crime car and Panda patrols. He thought you might like to get something on paper before you talk to him about it ... That's an invitation to talk to Rotary ... That's a Home Office conference on communications ... It mounts up, doesn't it?'

'I take it we're opting out of the crime business?'

'Sir?'

'Never mind.'

At half-past twelve he escaped to Teague's Eating House for lunch and he stayed there until two o'clock. There were no major cases on hand and he had no excuse for neglecting the routine administrative work. By six o'clock he was weary and bad tempered and he set out for home. The drizzle was so fine that it amounted to fog and he had to drive slowly. He was both puzzled and annoyed by the number of drivers who swished past him as though they were driving in bright sunshine.

'Well, what's it been like – first day back?' Helen took his coat.

'I was only away four days and that included the weekend.'

Helen laughed. 'You don't have to defend yourself to me.' She added, after a moment, 'Zelah rang.'

'Oh? What did she want?'

'The TV people are going to serialise one of her books – the one about Fanny Burney. I think it was called *Doctor's Daughter* or something like that.'

'I don't know, I didn't read it.'

'Anyway, she's on top of the world.'

'Good for her.'

He washed and changed his jacket before going into the living-room. Helen poured him a dry sherry.

'Zelah also said to tell you that they're now saying that the undertaker was murdered.'

'Then they'd better find his body.'

Helen grinned. 'You are in a mood! Anyway, I'm only passing

on her message. According to the gossip he was the Scapegoat in the Wheel on Saturday night. At least two people say they heard him scream.'

'People will say anything.'

'Is it so impossible?'

He picked up the *Radio Times* and glanced through the evening's programmes.

'I don't suppose it's impossible that he was in the thing, but as to screaming, don't you think he left it a bit late?'

'I suppose he could have been drugged.'

'Apart from all that, if somebody heard him scream, why did they wait till now to say so?'

'Don't ask me.'

'All right, I won't, but I hope Zelah hasn't got it into her head that I'm to do something about all this nonsense.'

'I don't think so, she was just passing on gossip.'

'Good.'

A delicious goulash served with a half-bottle of a light, fruity wine had a civilising influence. He made the coffee and helped with the washing up. Helen returned to the subject of the undertaker.

'I suppose if the local police thought there was anything in it they would be in touch with you as a matter of course.'

'If they thought a crime had been committed, but there's no crime in a man going missing.'

Back in the living-room Helen settled down to read while he dabbled with a crossword.

The telephone rang and he answered it.

He was speaking for some time and when he had finished he turned to his wife.

'That was Curtis, the CID man down there. They've found the undertaker's clothes all tied up in a neat bundle in a shed on the moor.'

'All his clothes?'

'All that he's likely to have been wearing, including shoes.'

'It looks bad, then?'

'Not good. There's a fair amount of blood on some of it.'

'Poor man! Shall you go down?'

37

'I suppose so.'

He was standing with his back to the fire, thinking how much less pleasant it would be in some seaside hotel or boarding house in the off-season.

'Tonight?'

'No. I'll ring Bourne and get him to organise a small team. We'll go down in the morning.'

'You could stay with the Ballards; Zelah would love that.'

'You must be joking! In any case the shed where the stuff was found can't be far from their place. If the chap was murdered Zelah may be a prime suspect.'

Helen chuckled. 'I can't think of anything that would please her more than to be investigated by you.'

'God forbid!'

Chapter Three

WHEN WYCLIFFE ARRIVED next morning the town was shrouded in a fine mist with a salty tang. From time to time the air glowed with a watery brilliance as though the sun might break through, but always the mists returned. The fog-horn on the lighthouse moaned at intervals, a surpassingly dismal sound like a cow in labour. Wycliffe left his car on the first car park he came to and walked. When he was starting on a case he used his car as little as possible. 'You see very little from a car or a desk,' he once said. 'It's like looking through the wrong end of a telescope.'

Although he was no stranger to the town, now that he was on a case he was seeing it with new eyes. He walked down the steep hill from the car park between rows of boarding houses which seemed to prop each other up against the slope: stone-built houses with bay windows, tiny front gardens and the inevitable signboards – SEA-VIEW, HILLSIDE, BELLA VISTA, MALABAR . . . OVERNIGHT ACCOMMODATION AND EVENING MEAL. The houses gave way to shops and the slope levelled off, then he was in a narrow main street where it was easily possible to hop on one leg from one gift shop to the next . . . all of them closed until Easter.

He knew that the police station was tucked away in a square behind the main street, next to a school.

It was a delightful little square; there was a great tree in the middle, a chestnut whose branches almost spanned the distance across it. The tree had survived because the square was too small to be taken seriously as a car park, and to make quite sure, some public-spirited individual had painted yellow lines round it. All the same, when Wycliffe arrived, there were three vehicles parked on the opposite side of the square from the police station; two were blue vans carrying the badge of the area police force, while the third belonged to the telephone engineers.

The police vans had been despatched from headquarters very early that morning and contained the equipment for setting up a temporary incident room. The divisional inspector had told him on the telephone of arrangements made for the use of a former Salvation Army hall, opposite the nick.

'It'll be very convenient, sir, though it's no palace – not by any means. But I will say this, it's a great deal better than it looks from the outside.'

Looking at the crumbling plaster, the sagging roof and murky little windows, Wycliffe hoped that the inspector was right.

From the school came the sound of children's voices singing a hymn, accompanied by a piano that was out of tune.

Curtis, the local CID sergeant, was waiting for him in the police station. Curtis was a very large man whose tiny facial features seemed lost in a desert of moist, granular skin. He was a man of few words but many graphic gestures. He nodded across the square. 'Your chaps have arrived, sir.'

Wycliffe filled his pipe and lit it. 'I heard something about this chap disappearing when I was here at the weekend. Do you really think he's been murdered?'

'Yes.'

Wycliffe liked that, no ifs or buts.

'All right, tell me about him.'

Curtis put him in the picture; his large, powerful hands seemed to tear vivid images out of thin air. 'I've known him all my life. Lean, lanky chap with skin like china-clay and a face like a horse.' His hands sketched an enormously over-developed chin. 'They call him the undertaker and, my God, it suited him. Black hair, dark suit and that resigned, gloomy look – smug, like he knows it's going to be your turn next.'

'He wasn't only an undertaker, was he?'

'Undertaker, builder, contractor, decorator ... Quite a big business, with contracts all over this part of the country.' The hands sketched architectural constructions which might have ranged from Ilium's topless towers to the semi-detached next door. 'Built it all out of nothing. His father was a shop assistant with old Toby Collins, the ironmonger.' Curtis added after a moment, 'I've got all his clobber spread out in the charge room.'

Each article was laid out on a polythene bag, labelled, ready to be sent to the laboratory. Wycliffe worked through the items. A dark-brown raincoat, grey sports jacket, grey trousers, woollen singlet, short pants, nylon socks and a grey, silk tie.

'Look, sir, there's a small bloodstain on the back of the singlet near the neck, but the shirt took most of it.'

The shirt was placed separately and Curtis jabbed at it with a thick, square forefinger.

'Most of it was sopped up by the double thickness of the collar at the back but it soaked down through. He couldn't have bled a great deal, perhaps a cupful all told. There are bloody smears over the rest of the shirt, as though somebody rolled it up before it was dry.'

Wycliffe looked closely at what appeared to be scorch marks on the collar where the blood had caked most thickly.

'Try the lens, sir.' Curtis passed him a hand-magnifier.

Among the fibres of the material it was easy to make out tiny, translucent granules of unburnt, smokeless powder.

'A bullet fired at close range into the back of the neck,' Wycliffe said. 'Is that what you make of it?'

Curtis shrugged.

The window of the charge room was high up in the wall, but through it Wycliffe could distinctly hear the strident voice of a woman teacher talking to her class. He picked up the sports jacket and examined the collar but could see no blood, no unburnt powder and no scorching.

'Same with the raincoat and tie, sir; clean, both of 'em.'

It was easy to imagine the undertaker sitting, relaxed, without his jacket or tie, being shot by someone behind him; probably by someone well known to him whose presence gave him no concern.

'I suppose a relative has checked this stuff?'

'His sister, Sarah, who keeps house for him. She reckoned this was what he was wearing when he left home Friday evening.'

'Nothing missing?'

'According to her, a peaked cap in a fine black-and-white check, a pair of kid gloves and his wrist watch. She says there must be money missing too.'

'Much?'

Curtis's hands contrived to suggest a modest sum. 'Say forty pounds.'

'And all this was found in a shed on the moor. Who found it?'

'Kids. Four boys, one of them the son of PC Eva. Mucking about on the moor like kids will, one of 'em went into the shed and came out with a bundle, all nicely tied up. They used it as a football for a bit – until it fell apart, then they saw the blood and got scared. They left the stuff where it was and scarpered but Terry Eva told his dad.'

'You don't think the kids took the money?'

Curtis pouted his thick lips. 'I know those kids; I'd bet against it.'

He walked over to another table where the contents of the undertaker's pockets had been laid out. A pocket handkerchief, a bunch of keys, sixty pence in coin, a pencil, a ball-point pen, a small piece of white chalk and a button. A leather wallet lay open with its contents exposed and itemised: business cards, driving licence, cheque book, banker's card and a few stamps.

'Sarah told me that he never went out without several pounds in his wallet and, in any case, he should have had the week's housekeeping money on him. He drew it each Friday when he drew the men's wages but he never handed the money over to Sarah until Saturday morning when she was off to do the shopping.' Curtis grinned. 'Couldn't bear to part with it until the last minute.'

It was unlikely that murder had been committed for a few pounds, but one could never be sure.

'We shall have to talk to his bank manager. Now we'd better get all this stuff off to the labs, but there's no point in sending his keys – we shall need them.'

Curtis was staring at the bloodstained shirt, 'I suppose it has to have been a firearm, sir?'

'What else?'

'Not a shotgun fired at very close range?'

'Impossible, I should think; the shot would have to be very tightly bunched to miss the material altogether and still have it scorched by the blast. In any case, a shotgun fired into the undertaker's neck at close range would have made a real mess; we wouldn't be looking at just a cupful of blood. What's on your mind?'

Curtis raised his shoulders in a slow shrug as though to establish a disclaimer in advance.

'There must be thirty or forty shotguns in this neighbourhood, sir, but there are only two firearms on our books, one revolver and one automatic.'

Wycliffe looked at him with greater attention. 'Out with it.'

'Gossip, sir.'

'I'm all for gossip.'

'I'm thinking of Timothy Jordan, a strange little man, a widower – '

'Jordan? The chap who organised the Fire Festival?'

'That's the man. He has a small-holding on the moor. Daughter recently had a child; father a question mark but gossip says it's the undertaker.'

'Why the undertaker?'

'She worked in his office.'

'So?'

'Jordan owns a shotgun and all this – ' he indicated the undertaker's clothing – 'all this was found in a shed within two hundred yards of his cottage.'

'But even if Riddle was the child's father, to shoot him would be over-reacting, wouldn't it?'

Curtis nodded. 'You'd think so. We live in a permissive society. God help us! A father doesn't go after his daughter's seducer with a shotgun – not any more.'

'Well, does he?'

Curtis smoothed the bristles on his chin. 'I'll admit it's gone out of fashion – not done any longer. But I doubt if anybody has ever told Timmy Jordan; he lives in the past.'

'You make him sound like a nut-case.'

Curtis took time to consider his reply. 'I wouldn't say that; he's a man with unusual views on a lot of things but he's no fool;

he goes round lecturing to Old Cornwall Societies, Women's Institutes and that sort of thing.'

'And he's at the top of your list?'

'No, I didn't say that, sir. I'm just passing on gossip for what it's worth.'

Wycliffe smiled. 'As I heard the gossip, Riddle replaced the Scapegoat in the Wheel and two witnesses heard him scream as he bowled down the hill.'

'I was coming to that bit, sir.'

Wycliffe was beginning to feel sure that he would enjoy working with Curtis. He said: 'Riddle went missing on Friday evening; when did his family report it to the police?'

'Sarah, his sister, phoned me at home on Sunday morning. I thought at the time she sounded a bit over anxious to explain why she hadn't told us before, but it wasn't long before I knew why.' He paused, holding Wycliffe with the steady gaze of his tiny blue eyes. 'Shortly after Sarah's call I had a visit from Laura Passmore.'

His restless hands seemed to conjure an attractive woman out of nothing. 'Laura must be nearing forty – her daughter, Hilda, is sixteen – but you'd take her for no more than thirty-five. Recently she divorced her husband – Ernie Passmore. Nobody was surprised about that. Ernie is the original layabout, a specialist in milking Social Security; he's dedicated his life to it.'

'Anyway, Laura wanted to know if anybody had reported that the undertaker was missing.' Curtis's face was massively cunning. 'I asked her, politely, what it was to do with her though, of course, I knew well enough.'

Wycliffe waited to be told.

'She was going to marry the undertaker. It was supposed to be a great secret but ...' Curtis's hands conveyed the futility of trying to keep secrets.

They walked across the square together, to the little hall which was to be Wycliffe's base for the duration of the case. Sergeant Bourne, his administrative assistant, was there with three detective constables, doing their best to make it look like home.

Bourne was young, one of the newer breed of policemen; a

graduate and mildly contemptuous of most things antedating the computer. Wycliffe, while conceding his abilities, saw no reason why he should also like him.

'We've got basic furniture, equipment and stationery; the telephone people are here and the gas people are coming to fix up radiators.'

Bourne was standing on a raised dais at one end of the hall under a text which read: 'By grace ye are saved.' He saw Wycliffe looking up at it. 'We'll get that thing down, sir.'

'Why? Don't you believe it?'

Bourne ignored that. 'Of course, the place is filthy and we are only able to clean up superficially.'

Wycliffe shrugged.

A constable brought a large-scale town map, which Bourne pinned to the match-boarding with which the walls were lined.

'Has Mr Scales arrived yet?'

'Not yet, sir, but he's on his way.'

Inspector Scales was one of the most able members of Wycliffe's team.

Wycliffe asked Curtis to point out Riddle's yard on the map.

'It's in Stockholm Backs, a few steps from the art gallery which is marked here, sir.'

'Who is likely to be in charge there?'

'Matthew Choak, Sarah's son. There's nobody else capable of running the place.'

'What sort of chap is he?'

'Thirtyish. Must know his job else Riddle wouldn't have kept him, nephew or no nephew. He's had a thin time. On the other hand, I don't think he'll get far without uncle's boot behind him.'

Wycliffe stood on the dais, smoking his pipe and looking round. It was a familiar scene, which had been repeated in dozens of rooms and halls throughout the police area; the same old battered filing cabinets and rickety tables; chipped metal trays and typewriters which had withstood the assaults of a generation of heavy handed coppers. Even the smell was coming right. Somewhere a telephone rang. They were in business.

'You've done a good job, Bourne.'

'Thank you, sir.' But he hardly sounded gratified.

Wycliffe turned to Curtis. 'I want you to get on to your divisional headquarters and ask them to organise a search of the moor in the neighbourhood of Jordan's farm. I doubt very much whether it will yield anything but it has to be done.'

'Do you want me on the search, sir?'

'No. I want you about here. Your first job will be to take one of these detective constables and, starting from Riddle's house, try to trace his movements on Friday evening. Use your imagination; somebody must have seen him.'

He turned to Bourne. 'I shall be at Riddle's yard.'

His way took him through narrow alleys, between rows of little granite cottages whose front doors opened to the street. It was not raining, but droplets of moisture condensed on every cold surface and Wycliffe could taste the salt on his lips. The fog-horn, its sound now muffled by the houses, continued to bleat at regular intervals. The names on the blue and white enamelled street signs intrigued him: Wesley Street, Zion Square, Temperance Place. They led him, inconsequently, to Stockholm Backs, where Riddle had his yard.

The newly painted double doors stood open to the yard, where a timber-lorry was being unloaded. A circular saw screeched and the smell of fresh sawdust was everywhere. He crossed the yard to a flat-roofed building labelled 'Office'.

A young girl with dark hair and a pert manner came to the enquiry window.

'Mr Matthew? He's in the office but he's busy.'

Wycliffe handed her his official card. 'Give him that, please.'

An older woman bustled over. 'What is it, Pat?' She took his card. 'Oh, the police, you'd better come in.'

She escorted him into an inner office where a young man sat behind a very large desk. He had papers in front of him, but Wycliffe felt sure that he had not been working. He was thin, dark and sallow, with prominent brown eyes, and he could have passed anywhere as a Lebanese or a Palestinian. He stood up, waving a long, limp hand.

Wycliffe was sympathetic. 'It must be a worrying and distressing time for you, Mr Choak.'

'It is. I can't think what can have happened to my uncle.' He swivelled to and fro in the padded chair.

'Well, that's what we have to find out, and you can help. You worked and lived with him, so you must know him better than most.'

It was obvious that Matthew would have been more at home at the little desk by the window, where there was only a kitchen chair to sit on. He was very nervous; he gathered together the papers on the desk.

'Apart from anything else, it's an impossible situation from a business point of view. What happens on Friday when we have to pay out wages?'

'Only Mr Riddle can sign cheques, is that it?'

Matthew gave a short, humourless laugh. 'You bet only Mr Riddle can sign cheques. I've been working here for fourteen years but I can't buy postage stamps without his say-so.'

Wycliffe could imagine the young man with his uncle – nervously polite, anxious to please, secretly resentful.

'I suppose your uncle has a solicitor?'

'Mr Penver of Cox, Penver and Green. He rang just now and I'm due to go round there this morning.'

'Then let's hope you will be able to sort something out. In the meantime, I have some questions. When did you last see your uncle?'

'On Friday afternoon, when we made the rounds of all our sites with the men's wages . . .'

'He paid them himself?'

'Always; it was a weekly ceremonial. Anyway, we arrived back here just before five and he asked me to keep an appointment he had made with Harry Collins at The Bay View. We've got the contract to convert the place into holiday flats and Collins wanted to talk over our arrangements for doing the work. I knew it would take some time, so I asked my uncle to tell mother I wouldn't be home for a meal. I was going out afterwards, you see.'

Wycliffe sensed some constraint in the young man's manner. 'Was this a quite normal thing for your uncle to do?'

Matthew's brown eyes were everywhere; occasionally they met Wycliffe's only to flit away again.

'It was quite usual for me to take on this sort of job but it wasn't usual for him to make an appointment for me and only tell me at the last minute, especially when it meant working after hours. It struck me as odd at the time, and when Harry Collins told me that he had asked for a morning appointment it seemed even odder.'

'What are you trying to tell me, Mr Choak?'

'Just that it looked as though he wanted me out of the way.'

'Why should he want that?'

'I've no idea.'

'What time did you get home after keeping your appointment with the hotelier?'

'About seven.'

'And your uncle had already gone out?'

'No, he was in his room and I didn't see him. I changed and left again within twenty minutes.'

'Where did you go?'

'I went to see a film at Penzance.'

'You drove over in your car?'

'Yes.'

At his little desk by the window he would be tolerated as long as nobody important came in, but when Riddle's visitor wanted to discuss real business it would be, 'If you don't mind, Matthew . . .' and Matthew would have to go.

'Were you alone?'

'Yes, there was nobody with me.' He seemed to think more was required. 'They were showing a film called *Straw Dogs*, which was made near here so I was interested.'

Wycliffe took out his pipe. 'May I?'

Matthew flushed. 'Of course!'

'What time did you get back to the house?'

He frowned. 'I was very late. My car – it's a van, actually – is old and not very reliable. I had a breakdown and didn't get back until half-past two or later. I went straight to bed but, of course, I didn't know that my uncle wasn't home.'

'Did your mother wait up for you?'

'No.'

'Tell me about the breakdown.'

'Well, when I was about two miles from Penzance the engine stopped and wouldn't start again. I couldn't find what was wrong and in the end I gave up and started to walk home. Two or three cars passed me and I tried to thumb a lift, but they didn't stop. Then it began to rain hard and I sheltered for a long time in a barn, but I couldn't stay there all night so I just walked and got thoroughly soaked. It was half-past two by the time I made it.'

He gave a wan smile.

'Your mother told Sergeant Curtis that Riddle left home at half-past seven on Friday evening to go to the yard; was that unusual?'

'No, he often went back to the yard in the evenings and almost always on Friday evenings. He said that he liked to square up the week's work.'

'When did you learn that your uncle had not come home?'

'At breakfast on Saturday. Mother asked me to call him, but he wasn't in his room and his bed hadn't been slept in.'

'The fact that your uncle was missing wasn't reported to the police until Sunday morning – isn't that rather odd?'

Matthew pursed his lips. 'Not if you knew uncle: he hated to have his movements watched or questioned. He'd have been very angry if he'd come back and found the police looking for him.'

One of the girls was on the telephone in the outer office: 'I'm afraid Mr Riddle isn't available at the moment ... No, I can't say when he will be back ... Mr Choak is running the business in his absence ... Very well, thank you.'

'The clothes which were found have been identified as your uncle's, but have you or your mother checked to see that no others are missing?'

'Mother checked. Sergeant Curtis was very particular about that. As far as she could tell, everything was there except his cap and gloves.'

Wycliffe said nothing and Matthew went on: 'I suppose,

what with the blood and everything, there's little chance of him being alive?'

'It looks bad, but at the moment we have no proof that the blood is your uncle's.'

Wycliffe was puzzled; the young man had answered his questions concisely and without hesitation, almost as though he was repeating a well-learned lesson, yet what he said was reasonable and credible.

'According to gossip, your uncle was substituted for the Scapegoat in Saturday's festival.'

Matthew shrugged. 'Nobody believes that, Mr Wycliffe.'

'Then why do they say it?'

'Because it makes a good story, something to talk about in the pubs.'

'They also say that he was murdered because he was the father of Cissie Jordan's baby.'

Matthew straightened his uncle's blotting pad. 'I've lived here all my life, Mr Wycliffe, and I've grown up with such tales; nobody takes them seriously.'

'Instant folklore, is that it?'

He smiled faintly. 'Something like that.'

Wycliffe's pipe was drawing nicely and he sat relaxed, as though he might stay indefinitely. Matthew became increasingly restive. There was something in his attitude which worried Wycliffe but he could not put a finger on it. It was almost as though the young man was preoccupied, troubled by some other problem or aspect which they had not touched upon.

'As far as you know, was your uncle in any financial difficulty?'

'I shouldn't think so for one minute but I don't know for certain.'

'You do not have access to the books?'

'Only to the day-to-day records which are kept here. The firm's accounting is done by a chap called Hooper – Morley Hooper. He's a retired accountant who is glad of the extra income. He looks after the preparation of the balance sheet and deals with the tax inspector.'

'Does he work here, in the office?'

'He spends a couple of days a month here, but the rest of the time he works at his home.'

Whenever they stopped talking the muffled sound of the machinery in the workshop seemed to become louder. In addition, Wycliffe could hear quite clearly what was happening in the outer office – the clacking of a typewriter, the girls exchanging scraps of conversation.

'That partition must be very thin.'

Matthew smiled. 'Uncle likes to keep himself informed.'

'But it must work both ways.'

'Uncle always speaks very quietly.'

'Mr Choak, you say that it is unlikely that your uncle was involved with the girl Jordan, but do you know of any other woman with whom he associated?'

Matthew played with the heavy desk ruler. 'He was planning to get married.'

'So I've been told. Was this something recent or something you have known about for a long time?'

'I heard it for the first time on Saturday morning.'

'After your uncle had disappeared?'

'Yes. Apparently he had told my mother and grandmother on Friday evening while they were having their meal.'

'Was it news to them?'

He hesitated. 'I think mother had her suspicions.'

'Did it come as a great surprise to you?'

Another pause. 'Yes and no. I suppose I have always thought of it as a possibility but his actual decision to marry was a surprise.'

'An unpleasant one?'

He rolled the ruler across the blotting pad. 'I've worked for fourteen years in this business and I've been given to understand that I should get a partnership one day.'

'And now?'

He looked up as though the question had startled him. 'I don't understand.'

'If your uncle has been murdered what do you expect to happen to the business and to you?'

'That depends on his will.'

51

'And has he never discussed his will with you?'

'Never. At the most he dropped hints that if I did my job and toed the line he would look after me.'

'Apart from the woman he was going to marry are you aware of any others in your uncle's life?'

'No, I don't think he associated with women.'

It all sounded straightforward – laudable even, and yet ...

'Just one more question, Mr Choak. Why are you so worried?'

He looked up, even paler if that were possible, and his fingers trembled on the ruler. 'I would have thought that my uncle's death ...'

'You might be distressed by your uncle's death; my word was *worried.*'

'But the whole responsibility of the business falls on me and I've no authority ... I explained ...'

'I think your worries are more personal.'

'I don't know what you're talking about.'

Wycliffe stood up, thanked him for his help and moved to the door.

'Don't bother to see me out.' After half-an-hour with him Wycliffe felt that he was as far from making an assessment as ever.

'Mr Wycliffe ...'

'Yes?'

'Nothing.'

'I think you have something to tell me.'

'No.' Matthew had his eyes fixed on the desk and did not look up. 'I was going to say that I don't know of anybody who could have killed my uncle.'

Wycliffe passed through the general office with a word to the two girls and stood for a while in the yard while the timber-lorry drove away and the big double doors were closed behind it. He was not consciously watching, but turning over in his mind what he had just heard, so that he was surprised to find the little brunette from the office standing at his elbow. She was obviously unsure of her reception.

'I don't suppose it's important, but I thought I ought to tell you that I saw Mr Riddle on Friday evening.'

She had innocent, dark-blue eyes and a cupid's-bow mouth which would certainly get her into trouble one day.

'I was out with my boyfriend and we passed him in Albert Terrace.'

'Where is that?'

'Not far from where he lives.'

'Was he going towards his house or away from it?'

'Away from it. I suppose he was going down the hill to Moorgate Road, there's nowhere else to go from Albert Terrace.'

'What time was this?'

She thought. 'It must have been between half-past seven and eight.'

'Did he speak?'

'Well, I said "Goodnight, Mr Riddle" and he answered. He didn't say anything.'

'Did he seem just as usual?'

'Yes. Like he is, only half noticing you except when he wants something.' She tried to imitate the undertaker. '"Goodnight, Miss . . ." all stiff and starchy. But that's how he is, he never lets go.'

'After he passed you, did you notice whether he went into one of the houses or continued down the hill?'

'Sorry, I didn't notice.'

'It doesn't matter.'

The blue eyes watched him; she was eager to be questioned.

'Did you replace Cissie Jordan?'

'No, I worked here with Cissie. We're one short at the moment.' She gave him a knowing look. 'I suppose you're thinking about all the gossip – about Riddle being the baby's father?'

'Has Mr Riddle ever made any advances to you?'

'I'd like to see him try.'

'You don't believe the gossip, do you?'

She frowned and shook her head. 'No. I didn't like him, he used to give me the creeps, but he wasn't that sort.'

'What about Matthew?'

'He's too frightened to do much.'

'Why do they keep those double doors closed?'

She was surprised by the sudden change of subject but she answered readily enough.

'That's him again – the boss. He really gets steamed up if they're left open, you'd think somebody was going to run off with the timber mill.'

'Thanks.'

'Is that all?'

'For the moment.'

She was disappointed. 'Could I have your autograph?' She held out the pad she had been holding.

He signed his name.

'Write Detective Chief whatever it is.'

'I'll leave you to do that.'

She shrugged, then scurried off back to the office, showing a lot of thigh.

He walked back by a different route which took him along the waterfront. The mist still limited visibility to less than a hundred yards and the fog-horn continued to blare at regular intervals. The children were having their eleven o'clock break, but as Wycliffe entered the square the ringing of a bell cut off the cacophony of sound as though at the flick of a switch. Back in the hall, he was delighted to see that John Scales had arrived.

Scales was the most imaginative of his inspectors; he had started in fingerprints and now specialised in fraud cases. He dressed well and had the voice and manners to match, so that accountants, bank managers and lawyers tended to forget that he was a policeman and sometimes let down their guard.

Wycliffe greeted him with warmth.

'I assume that you're in the picture, John?'

'More or less, sir.'

'Two jobs for you. First the manager of London and Provincial, where Riddle banked. He drew wages for his firm on Friday; did he draw any other monies and if so, how much?'

'Do I tell him that we assume Riddle to be dead?'

'You can give that impression without actually saying so.

54

Also, and this is more tricky, we want to know what Riddle's financial position is. Is there any chance that he's done a moonlight in order to get away from money problems?'

'Is that on the cards, sir?'

'I don't think so but we need to be sure. It's no good looking for a man's body round here if the owner's living it up in Costa Rica. The evidence we've got so far could have been manufactured.'

'You said you had two jobs for me, sir.'

'Yes, the other is to see Riddle's solicitor – Mr Penver, of Cox, Penver and Green. Discreet enquiries about his affairs, particularly any will he may have made or altered. At the same time I'd be glad of his views on Matthew Choak, the nephew who now runs the business.'

'I get the message, sir.'

Scales left and Wycliffe called Sergeant Bourne over.

'Any more men arrived?'

'Sergeant Smith and Detective Constables Dixon and Fowler came down with Mr Scales, sir.'

'Good! Send one of them to talk to this chap Jordan – Fowler will do it very well; he'd have been more than a match for the Ancient Mariner. I don't want him to lean on Jordan at this stage, just open up the possibilities. Now, let's have another look at your map.'

In addition to the town plan there was now a six-inch Ordnance Survey map of the district pinned to the wall.

'What are these marks?'

'I'm making a key as we go along, sir. Number one is Riddle's house, two is his yard, three is Jordan's small-holding and four is the hut where the clothing was found.'

Wycliffe studied the street plan. 'Here we are, Albert Terrace. Riddle was seen there between half-past seven and eight on Friday night.'

Bourne made a mark on the map.

Wycliffe traced the route the undertaker must have taken. As the girl had said there was no way out of Albert Terrace except down the steep hill to the road by the shore. From there, to the left, a footpath led to the moor, while to the right, a road continued into the town. The footpath passed the shed where the boys had found Riddle's clothes, then joined a track which led to Jordan's farm. There could be no doubt that for a man on foot this was the quickest way from Riddle's house to Jordan's farm.

'One more thing – Matthew Choak told me that he went to Penzance on Friday night to see the film, *Straw Dogs*. It seems that he had a breakdown on the way back and had to walk. I want you to put Dixon on checking his story.'

'Does he have to do it without Choak knowing, sir?'

'It doesn't matter. Unless I'm mistaken Choak is accustomed to having his statements checked.'

'Do you mean he's got form?'

'No, only an uncle.'

Sergeant Curtis came in to report that a woman living near Riddle had seen him in Bay View Terrace on Friday evening, but this merely confirmed the route he had taken. Wycliffe told the sergeant what he had learned from the girl in Riddle's office and Curtis became animated.

'It's obvious! He must have been on his way to Jordan's place. Where else could he have been going? If he was going to the town he would have gone straight down Buller's Hill and been there in ten minutes.'

Wycliffe shook his head. 'You may be right but don't let's get hooked on one idea. Detective Constable Fowler is up at Jordan's place now.'

He re-lit his pipe, which had gone out.

'Look at it this way, Curtis: the boys discovered Riddle's clothes tied in a bundle in a shack near Jordan's cottage – right?'

Curtis nodded.

'If you'd put those clothes there would you have expected them to be found sooner or later?'

'Sooner rather than later. There's more activity on those moors than you might think.'

'Whoever put the clothes there might reasonably have expected that they would be found within a few days?'

'Yes.'

'So, if Jordan put them there he must have wanted them to be found – why? He could have disposed of them in a more conclusive way on a bonfire or by throwing them down an old mineshaft.'

Curtis grinned. 'I wouldn't put it past the old devil to have done it out of sheer bravado.'

'Maybe. But let's get back to police work. I want every house in Albert Terrace and any that lie between the terrace and the town checked. And remember that if Riddle was murdered on Friday night his killer is not going to be anxious to admit having had a visit.'

Chapter Four

WITHIN AN HOUR or so Bourne had equipped a little room off the dais as a private office for the chief superintendent. He was given a table, three chairs, a filing cabinet, letter trays and a telephone. In Bourne's view (shared by many of Wycliffe's high-ranking colleagues) it was from there that he should conduct the investigation, receiving reports, issuing instructions, discussing the case with his officers and, very occasionally, interrogating a witness himself. But he seemed reluctant even to enter the little room. For a long time he stood in front of the town map, gazing at it as though he would memorise its every feature, and when he turned away it was to ask for a cup of coffee.

Scales arrived back and it was only then that Wycliffe went into the office.

'Pull up a chair, John.'

Scales sat down, easing his trousers at the knees to avoid bagging. 'Riddle drew the usual wages from the bank on Friday, sir, but he also cashed a personal cheque for two hundred and ninety pounds.'

'I suppose that was exceptional?'

'Unprecedented. He usually drew forty pounds from his personal account each week so he must have needed two hundred and fifty for something.'

'In what denominations?'

Scales frowned. 'That's another odd thing. He insisted on used fivers. As it was Friday – wages day for most firms – the cashier was trying to conserve his stock of fivers and asked Riddle to take notes of larger denomination, but he refused and got quite irritable.'

'What about his general standing?'

'No problem; the manager was very co-operative. He said that Riddle's business was a sound concern with a steadily rising turnover and increasing profitability. Apart from re-investing in his own business Riddle has been buying industrial shares while the market is depressed, presumably on the assumption that there are better times ahead. The bank sees him as a sound and very shrewd business man . . .'

A constable brought Wycliffe's coffee; he sipped it and made a wry face.

'You should be used to it by now, sir.'

'Anything else?'

'One item. The manager was more cagey about this. Recently Riddle bought four fields which form part of a camping site at Miller's Bottom. The site is run by a chap called Sidney Passmore and I gather there's been a lot of ill-feeling.'

Wycliffe nodded. 'Curtis mentioned this Sidney. The woman Riddle was going to marry – Laura Passmore, was recently divorced from Sidney's brother, Ernie.'

Scales paused to take this in.

'Did you manage to see the lawyer?'

'I saw him but it didn't get me very far; he's one of the old and crusted. He admitted that Riddle had made a will three or four years back, and he thinks the provisions of that will stand, but he wouldn't tell me what they were. Under gentle pressure he conceded that Riddle had mentioned the possibility of marriage and said that in this circumstance he would want to make a fresh will.'

'Any views expressed about Master Matthew?'

'I tried the bank manager and the lawyer on that one and neither of them showed any enthusiasm. "I can't take to him; he seems a shifty customer to me," was the bank manager's verdict. Penver, the lawyer, more restrained, thought him unreliable.'

'Two hundred and fifty pounds in used notes looks very like blackmail but, for these days, it's a modest demand from a comparatively wealthy man.'

'And if it was a pay-off it didn't do him any good.'

Wycliffe pushed his chair back with a show of irritation. 'I don't like murder cases without a body, John.' He stood up and stretched himself. 'You keep this perch warm for a while, I'm doing a walkabout.'

He stepped out into the square and lit his pipe just as a watery sun broke through the clouds. Was the undertaker being blackmailed? Wycliffe had doubts, but he had no doubt that he was dead.

He walked through a narrow alley into the main street and stood on the corner by a butcher's, looking up and down. Even in November it was a busy little town, though a good third of the shops were closed until the spring.

Presumably several people would benefit very substantially from Riddle's will, but how would his projected marriage have changed that? God knows, the threat of a changed will is a hoary old chestnut as a motive for murder but it remains a perfectly good one. He was not impressed by all the hocus-pocus with the Scapegoat nor by the gossip which linked Jordan with the dead man, but beyond all that he was beginning to feel – to sense – that this was a sinister crime, an expression of hatred, long nurtured in secret until it could no longer be contained.

He walked up the main street for a hundred yards and came to a road off on his right labelled Buller's Hill. He remembered that Riddle's house was known as Buller's Hill House and decided to go in search of it.

If, and it was a very big 'if', Riddle's body had been substituted for the Scapegoat he felt sure that it was not as a convenient way of disposing of the body but to give more effective expression to the hatred which had inspired his killing. The man had been stripped naked and his clothes left, tied in a bundle, for children or lovers to find.

At first there was no hill but a street of small shops; greengrocer, baker, ironmonger, decorator, confectioner ... Then the shops gave place to boarding houses and the hill began; it was a twin of the one he had come down from the car park.

These were the people Wesley had come to Cornwall to save, to rescue from the devil and, by all accounts, they had given the old campaigner a hard time of it.

The hill seemed to go on and on. Most of the houses exhibited 'No Vacancy' signs – not because they were full but because they did not want to be bothered by the stray dogs of winter.

Buller's Hill – presumably named after General Sir Henry Redvers Buller, the man who relieved Ladysmith. Wycliffe remembered a great-uncle who had fought under Buller and talked of little else. Now hardly anybody remembered him and many had never heard of Ladysmith.

Wycliffe prided himself on being reasonably fit, but by the time he was halfway up the hill he knew that he had a heart and lungs.

A bachelor of nearly fifty decides to marry. Over the years he has woven an intricate pattern of life in private and in business; he has established a system of relationships which has the merit that it works. Now he proposes to throw in a wife. Wycliffe chuckled to himself at the picture he had conjured up.

It was important to find out whether Riddle's body could have been in the Wheel and, if it could, was it possible for anyone other than Jordan to have put it there? At least, he supposed that it was important, but he could not work up any enthusiasm. It was too dramatic, too pat. If the evidence meant anything Riddle had died of a bullet fired into his neck, not of a stake driven through his heart.

All the same . . .

He was nearing the top of the hill and turned to look at the view as an excuse for a breather. The mist had finally gone and there was sunshine on the water. It was too perfect; a picture postcard blown up to the scale of real life. The bay, the promontories, the little white pencil of a lighthouse stuck on its rock. Pine trees somewhere in the foreground, open enough to see through but framing the picture. He wanted to do more than just look; it was at such times that he felt the urge to paint.

Buller's Hill House came as a surprise. He was not prepared for anything so impressive. Gravelled drive and laurels, Gothic gables, chimneys and windows. Wycliffe wished that he had known the undertaker.

He sighed as he rang the front doorbell. 'What the hell am I playing at?'

Sarah answered the door; she wore a shabby blue woollen dress, her grey hair straggled and she looked as though she could do with a wash. She was a big woman, tall and gaunt, and she spoke with a gruff, masculine voice.

'Another policeman?'

'I'm afraid so. Detective Chief Superintendent Wycliffe.'

'You'd better come in.'

The drawing-room was gloomy and overpowering, with lots of dark, fretted woodwork, red plush upholstery and a huge carpet square with a Persian design almost obscured by in-grained dirt. A small coal fire burned in the grate.

'Well, have you found him?'

Wycliffe was startled by the question, which did not come from Sarah but from an old lady who sat on the far side of the fire. Wycliffe had not seen her at first. She sat bolt upright; her features were strong, her manner forthright, even aggressive.

Sarah said, 'My mother.' She pointed to a chair.

'I asked you if you'd found him.'

'I'm afraid not.'

'Is it true that you're going after Timmy Jordan?'

Wycliffe took refuge in an official cliché. 'We are looking into all the possibilities.'

The old lady made a disparaging noise. 'Gossip! Only fools listen to gossip. You're not a fool – or are you?'

'I hope not.'

Her steady brown eyes regarded him. 'So do I. I want you to find whoever murdered my son. I suppose you're the top man?'

'I'm in charge of this investigation.'

'Good! Well, I'll tell you one thing; whoever killed him it wasn't Timmy Jordan, he's crack-brained but he's harmless.'

'There is no conclusive proof that your son is dead.'

She ignored the interruption. 'Jonathan did well enough in business, but he was too easy in other ways. Weak. Unless I'm very much mistaken, there's a woman at the back of this.'

'Mother, you've no reason to –'

'You hold your tongue, Sarah!'

'I understand that Mr Riddle was planning to marry.'

The old lady nodded. 'So you've heard. Laura Passmore, and if you're going to tell me she had no reason to want him dead, you may be right. But she only came on the scene recently; there were others. Jonathan wasn't what you'd call a warm man but he wasn't a monk either. You understand me?'

'I think so. But have you anybody in mind? Let me put it differently. Do you suspect or know that your son was involved with any particular woman?'

'I don't know who she is but I know that she exists.'

'On what evidence?'

'I'm his mother and I knew him.'

He turned to Sarah. 'Is that your opinion also, Mrs Choak?'

Sarah had to clear her throat before answering. 'I don't go in for crystal gazing.'

Wycliffe tried another line.

'One of my men talked to Mr Penver this morning.'

The old lady snorted. 'He won't tell you anything, he's a mealy-mouthed old hypocrite.'

'But your son's will may be important to the case and I shall be glad of your help to –'

'I can tell you what you want to know.'

Wycliffe saw the look of astonishment on Sarah's face; she turned to her mother, opened her mouth to speak but, apparently, changed her mind.

'You mean that you know the contents of his will?'

'Near enough. He discussed it with me when he made it and he's talked about it since.' The old lady pulled her cardigan round her and fastened one of the buttons.

Sarah could no longer contain herself. 'You mean that you've known all along and never said a word –?'

Her mother turned on her. 'His will was his own business; he'd have told you if he wanted you to know. Anyway, the house comes to me.' Her lips parted in a small smile which she could not control. 'You have the right to live here, Sarah, as long as you want and it will be yours when I'm gone. Apart from that, the business is to be put on the market –'

'*Sold*?' Sarah's voice expressed utter incredulity.

'Sold, and the money put with his other assets and distributed.'

'What do you mean, *distributed*?' Sarah asked the question as though her life depended on the answer.

'According to the will, you get seven thousand.'

'And Matthew?'

'Two thousand, as far as I remember.'

'You mean that after slaving away for fourteen years all he gets is two thousand?'

'He was paid.'

'A pittance.'

'That's his fault. He should have had the guts to demand more or get out.'

Sarah was pale with anger. 'And what happens to the rest?'

'The residue of the estate comes to me.'

She reminded Wycliffe of a satiated cat, licking her lips.

Sarah snapped, 'I shall fight this, don't you think I shan't!'

The old lady shrugged.

Nobody spoke for a while and it was Sarah who eventually broke the silence. 'But what would have happened if you'd gone first? I mean, that's what he must have expected.'

'If I'd gone first, the house would have come to you with ten thousand and the rest would have gone for research into glandular diseases.'

'*Glandular diseases?*' Sarah was barely articulate. 'What are you talking about now? I don't believe it!'

'Suit yourself. He thought he was suffering from some sort of glandular disease. Of course, he only imagined it; he was as healthy as you or me.'

With nearly thirty years in the force Wycliffe had rarely felt so shamed by others. Most people in the circumstances would have refused to believe what the evidence told them. Not so here. In a few days Riddle's body might be found and the two women would almost certainly arrange an elaborate funeral which they would attend and shed a few crocodile tears.

'Did he discuss with you how his will would be affected by his intended marriage?'

'There was no time. No doubt he would have done.'

'I assume that your son, Matthew, knows nothing of the will?' Wycliffe had turned to Sarah.

'Certainly not, but he soon will, I promise you, and we shall be down seeing Penver first thing tomorrow morning.'

Wycliffe tried to imagine the undertaker with his two women. Was he cast in the same mould? And where did Matthew fit in? Was it a household so permeated by dislike and distrust that only the bald fact of dependence constrained them to preserve an uneasy peace?

'When did Mr Riddle tell you that he intended to marry?'

'On Friday evening when we were having our meal.'

'Were you greatly surprised?'

Sarah said, 'We'd heard rumours.'

'Did he discuss with you any of the changes it would entail?'

'He said that he wanted to sell this house, but he would buy a smaller one for mother and me. He was going to build a new place for her.'

'What time did he usually get home?'

Sarah frowned. 'It varied; sometimes before I went to bed, sometimes after.'

'What time did you go to bed on Friday night?'

'About eleven and, of course, he wasn't in.'

'What about your son?'

'Matthew wasn't in either. He went to the pictures in Penzance and his car broke down.'

At times in the past there must have been tenderness between the members of this family; the old lady had conceived and given birth to two children, nursed them and watched them grow into adult life. Sarah, in her turn, must have experienced something of the warmth of feeling which can link one human being to another, but now, all that was left was a fierce possessiveness, veined with jealousy which at any moment could flare into hatred.

'On the day Mr Riddle disappeared he drew two hundred and ninety pounds from his private account. That was quite exceptional; he usually drew only forty pounds and I am anxious to find out why he needed another two hundred and fifty.'

The two women were looking at him with great attention but it was the mother who spoke first. 'Doesn't that prove what I told you? There was a woman and he was paying her off.'

Although outside the sun was shining and this room was in the front of the house, no glimmer of sunlight filtered through the venetian blinds and the half-drawn curtains, only a dusty grey luminosity which seemed to chill the room.

'I suppose there is some place where he kept his papers and private things?'

They looked at him but did not answer at once.

'I need to go through them.'

'You'd better show him, Sarah.'

'This way.'

She led the way upstairs, past a stained-glass window in the style of Burne-Jones to a first-floor landing. Five or six mahogany doors opened off it and there was another flight of stairs.

'His bedroom is that room there; he preferred to sleep in the back. This is his office.'

She pushed open the door of a room overlooking the bay, a room flooded with sunshine but musty and stale. A flat-topped desk stood by the window. There was a telephone, a chair upholstered in worn, black leather and bookshelves full of faded dusty books. An electric fire stood in the fireplace and above it there was a large-scale Ordnance Survey map of the town and district.

'You'll have a job to see anything; he kept it all locked up. You'd think he was living in an hotel.'

'I've got his keys.'

'Oh.'

Wycliffe stood by the desk, Sarah planted herself in the doorway.

'I shall be here for some time.'

'I suppose if you find anything we shall be told?'

'Everything here will be available to Mr Riddle's lawyer and if I have to take anything away I shall give you a receipt.'

She said nothing to this but continued to stand in the doorway. 'I suppose you have an office in the police station?'

'No; in the old Salvation Army building opposite. Why do you ask?'

'I just wondered.' After a moment she went, closing the door behind her.

Wycliffe had a little room where he kept his books and papers, his photographs and odds and ends he valued. It had a desk, a chair, bookshelves and cupboards. The contents of that room had grown with him; they were an extension of his personality, intimate and revealing. As he sat in Riddle's chair he experienced a pang of conscience but also a guilty thrill. He was intensely interested in other people's inner lives; he read autobiographies, especially diaries, not as a *voyeur* but rather for reassurance. From childhood he had feared that his most intimate thoughts and desires were different from those of others and when his reading showed him that they were not he felt that his grip on life had been strengthened, his confidence reinforced.

The drawers of the desk were all locked but he had no difficulty in finding the right key. What he found in most of the drawers was of little immediate interest: personal bank statements, cheque book, an account book in which Riddle kept a record of his investments, another which itemised personal expenditure. Wycliffe put them all back where he had found them for Scales to look at. In another drawer there was a file of household bills and receipts for the current year.

In the large bottom drawer on that side there were two books – one, a medical encyclopedia and the other, a technical work on the human endocrine system. Certain passages in the encyclopedia and the textbook had been heavily marked: references to acromegaly and to malfunction of the pituitary gland.

'Treatment other than by X-rays or surgery to the pituitary gland has little or no effect ... The condition is due to excessive secretion of the so-called "growth hormone" by the pituitary gland ... The most obvious symptoms are *thickening of the skull, face, hands and feet* ... Complications sometimes arise as a result of internal organs being affected, these include diabetes and possible impotence ... Vision is sometimes impaired.

'Acromegalics are often unusually strong, but in later life the pituitary becomes exhausted and *the once strong man becomes flabby and weak.*'

Certain phrases had been doubly underlined.

The drawers on the other side contained stationery, pens and pencils, rubber bands and paper clips. It was again the bottom drawer in which he found most of interest. Riddle, a systematic person, had used it for all the oddments he had wished to keep which did not fit into his filing system, and the bottom of the drawer was covered to a depth of two or three inches with papers. Wycliffe lifted them out and started to sort through them. His task was made easier by the fact that the papers were clipped together in small bundles.

Many were newspaper cuttings, ranging in content from dietetic hints to stock market forecasts. One little package of manuscript papers intrigued and moved him; it was a collection of short poems, naïve and crude but full of loneliness and self-pity. A large envelope contained a photograph, evidently the original of a press photograph, of two men on a platform, one investing the other with a chain of office. A typewritten caption read: 'Mr Jonathan Riddle being invested as President of the Cornish Master Builders' Federation by the retiring President, Mr J.D. Chirgwin.'

Riddle was having to bend low to allow the chain to be passed over his head and he presented his profile to the camera at a grotesque angle which seemed to accentuate a protruding jaw, long nose and bony ridge over the eyes.

He almost missed another, smaller envelope, addressed to Riddle in a round, childish hand. The envelope contained a letter which he opened and read. It was dated three days before Riddle's disappearance.

Dear Mr Riddle,
I must talk to you privately. I don't want to come to your office or your house but I am alone in the office at the Fish Co-operative from twelve to one each day except Saturday. It is very important so I hope you will come.
                                        Yours truly,
                                        Hilda Passmore.
P.S. You must not mention this to my mother.

Wycliffe slipped the letter into his pocket.
He put the papers back into the drawer and locked the desk,

but continued to sit there. He had a clear picture of a sad and lonely man, deeply concerned about his health and dwelling on a future which seemed to promise only a fairly rapid decline into senility. Whether such pessimism was justified was hardly relevant ... He reached for the telephone directory and looked up the number of Morley Hooper, the retired accountant whom Matthew had told him looked after Riddle's more important business affairs. He dialled the number and waited. After a little while a man with a pleasant Cornish brogue answered: 'Morley Hooper.'

Wycliffe was diplomatic, but in the end he was encouraged by the man's attitude to put straight questions.

'I wondered if you also acted for him in his private affairs?'

'I did his personal tax return and kept an eye on his investments.'

'Obviously you do not have to answer at this stage if you would prefer not to, but I wondered if Mr Riddle had taken out any substantial life insurance or endowment policies?'

'I see no reason why I shouldn't answer that. He took out an endowment policy ten years ago to mature when he reached the age of sixty.'

'For a large sum?'

'Fifteen thousand pounds.'

'That sum also to be payable in case of death before the age of sixty?'

'Yes.'

Wycliffe thanked him and replaced the receiver. It was possible that Riddle had committed suicide in such a way as to make it appear that he had been murdered. In such circumstances the insurance would be paid in full. It seemed unlikely that the undertaker had troubled sufficiently about those who survived him to take such precautions, but no one could speak with confidence of what had passed through the mind of this man whose deepest preoccupations seemed to be represented by a few scored lines in a medical book and a little bundle of poems.

Wycliffe got up from the desk and crossed the landing to Riddle's bedroom. The room was gloomy, filled with massive, mahogany furniture and pervaded by a musty smell which seemed to characterise the whole house. The room contained nothing personal except for the dead man's clothes and these were carefully stored in the great wardrobe and the chest-of-drawers.

As he walked down the stairs it was the old lady who met him in the hall.

'Well?'

'Thank you for allowing me to go through his papers.'

'Did you find anything?'

'Nothing.'

'You'll keep me informed?'

'Of course.'

He was out in the sunshine, his feet crunching the gravelled drive with which Riddle had put the finishing touch to his little estate. He walked back to the square, preoccupied and disregarding the life of the town around him.

'Anything new?'

Scales got up from his seat at the table in Wycliffe's little office but Wycliffe waved him back.

'Dixon has been checking on Matthew Choak's trip to Penzance on Friday evening. The cinema was pretty full, so he couldn't get much there. However, one of our Panda drivers noticed a Mini van parked off the road in Badger's Cross at about one in the morning. The van was empty but he made a note of the number and it checks. It was Choak's vehicle and it was still there on Saturday morning.'

Wycliffe nodded. 'Keep Dixon on it. I want to know as much as possible about that young man and his movements. Is Fowler back?'

'I think he's gone for refreshments.'

Fowler, who arrived a few minutes later, was middle-aged; he had stayed a detective constable ostensibly because he could not pass the examination for sergeant, but his colleagues claimed that he deliberately avoided promotion. Certainly he lacked nothing in intelligence or skill.

'Well, how did you get on with Jordan?'

Fowler's eyes twinkled. 'It took the better part of an hour to get to brass tacks, but we managed it in the end, sir.'

Fowler had arrived at the small-holding around lunchtime. He had left his car on a muddy track some distance from the cottage which was scarcely visible through the mist. Seaward there was nothing but a pearly opalescence which, though it seemed likely to vanish at any moment, effectively blocked out sea and sky. Fowler looked at the tiny fields of black soil and wondered how anyone could scratch a living from them.

The yard in front of the cottage was littered with discarded buckets, an old bath, a mangle and a pile of driftwood. A few hens pecked between the cobbles and rabbits scuffled in hutches along one of the dry-stone walls. The cottage, with its lichen-covered roof, looked as though it had grown out of the moor.

He knocked on the plank half-door.

'Well?'

His knock was answered by a girl of seventeen or eighteen. She was attractive in a plump, slovenly way, with a mass of jet-black curls, dark eyes and brown skin. A Radio One disc jockey prattled in the background.

Fowler showed his warrant card. 'Police. I suppose you must be Cissie.'

She did not answer directly. 'I'll get father, he's seeing to the pigs.'

She went round the back of the cottage and returned a minute or two later followed by a stocky, white-haired man with lively, intelligent brown eyes and skin as dark as a gypsy's.

'Mr Jordan?'

'That's me. I suppose you've come about the undertaker. A strange business, isn't it? My word, yes; very strange.'

Fowler was taken into the kitchen and given a chair to one side of the cooking range while Jordan sat opposite him. Cissie sat on a kitchen chair by the table, reading; the pram, with her baby in it, was at her elbow. The window was so small that until his eyes became accustomed to the dim light Fowler could make out few details.

With skill borne of long practice he let the old man talk but guided his talk in the way he wanted it to go, then he started to ask questions.

'About the Wheel, Mr Jordan. I gather that you built it

yourself in one of your sheds and that it was there until Saturday afternoon, the day of the festival – is that right?'

Jordan nodded. 'Quite right.'

'Was the shed locked?'

'Locked? Why should I lock it? There's nothing to steal, is there? Nothing!' Jordan's conversation was sprinkled with questions which he usually answered himself, often with some approving comment.

'Was the Scapegoat already in place on Friday evening?'

'Oh, yes, the Wheel was ready for the ceremony except for the foliage; we do that on the day of the event so that it is fresh; laurel and yew. Laurel was sacred to Apollo and ...'

'How do you set about making the Scapegoat itself?'

Jordan looked at him with humorous eyes. 'You are asking the priest to betray the mysteries. I'm not sure that I should tell you, but seeing that you are a policeman ... We don't want trouble with the law, do we? Oh, dear me, no!'

There was something savoury cooking in the oven, and once or twice Cissie came over, opened the oven door and looked in. The fire burned silently except when the coals shifted and a shower of glowing ash filtered through to the tray below. Cissie took no part in the conversation; she seemed completely absorbed in her book. Occasionally the baby whimpered and she jiggled the handle of the pram until it stopped. A clock on the mantelpiece ticked loudly.

'The Scapegoat is made of any old bits of wood nailed together to form a trunk, legs and arms. The shape is made by tying on bundles of straw, and the garments help. The head is straw too, covered with a stocking and fitted with a mask and a hat. It's simple, really, like a guy on Guy Fawkes' day.'

'You make the Scapegoat quite separately and tie it on afterwards?'

'Oh, yes, it's tied by the "ankles" and "wrists" to the Wheel.'

'Now, Mr Jordan, would it have been possible for someone to get into your shed on Friday night, remove the Scapegoat and substitute a body dressed in the Scapegoat's clothes?'

Jordan laughed. 'You're not listening to that old yarn, surely? Believe me, Mr Fowler, the people round here make up these stories because they've nothing better to do in the winter. They don't believe them. Oh, dear, no!'

'I asked you a question, Mr Jordan.'

The clock on the mantelpiece, after a preliminary throat clearing, struck one.

'There you are, Cissie, time to feed the baby. Mustn't keep his lordship waiting. My word, no!'

Cissie, without a word, lifted the baby out of the pram on to her lap, pulled up her jumper and put the baby to her breast.

'Isn't that a beautiful picture, Mr Fowler? Warms a man's heart it does. Puts a meaning into life.'

'You were about to tell me if what I suggested could have happened.'

Jordan grinned. 'Of course it could have happened, but it didn't.'

'How do you know?'

Jordan spread his hands. 'Think of the difficulties, Mr Fowler. First, I don't see how one man could have managed it alone. He would have had to get the body up here –'

'Riddle might have come here of his own accord.'

'But why? Why should Mr Riddle come here? We had nothing in common – nothing.'

The brown eyes searched Fowler's face with more concern than they had yet shown. He was nobody's fool, but Fowler had been told to avoid scaring him.

'All I want to know is, if such a substitution was made would you have noticed it?'

Jordan, very serious now, reflected. 'I can't honestly say. There would have been a difference in weight, but we don't lift the Wheel at any stage, we roll it. I don't know.'

'How was it taken from here to the launching ramp?'

'On Jimmy Tregaskis's truck – he's a nurseryman and he's one of the committee who –'

'The two of you rolled it up planks on to the truck, roped it down and drove it to the site; is that right?'

'There were three of us, actually; Jimmy brought Morley Richards with him to lend a hand.'

'You took the Wheel to the site and set it up on the ramp; was it left unattended at any time?'

Jordan looked pained. 'What do you think, Mr Fowler? Would we leave a thing like that when any kiddy could knock the chocks out or set light to it? Of course we didn't leave it.'

There was silence, only the clock ticking and a little gurgling noise from the baby. Cissie was holding her baby with one hand and her book with the other.

'Watch him now, Cissie. We don't want him to get the wind, do we? No, my goodness, that would never do.'

Fowler had not yet heard a word from Cissie, which perhaps explained why the old man asked and answered his own questions.

Fowler was sitting by an alcove where there were shelves stuffed with books, old books with broken spines and faded lettering so that it was impossible to decide what most of them were about.

'Do you own a shotgun, Mr Jordan?'

'You must know that I do.'

'I would like to see the gun.'

Jordan went into his bedroom and came back with his gun. Fowler took it, opened the breech and looked down the twin barrels. The gun was clean and well-oiled, but in places the oil had begun to thicken and to collect dust.

'You don't appear to have used this for some time.'

'Not since early summer when I shot a couple of rooks to keep the birds off my peas.'

Fowler had been told not to press the old man, but the parentage of Cissie's baby had been the cause of much of the gossip.

'Well, Mr Jordan, thank you, that's all for the moment.' He stood up, hoping that Jordan would see him out.

It worked; the old man came with him into the junk-filled yard.

'I didn't want to raise this in front of your daughter, Mr Jordan, but had you any special reason to harbour a grudge against Riddle?'

75

'Special reason? No, I can't say that I had; like many others I simply disliked the man.'

Fowler tried again. 'In a case which looks like murder we are bound to listen to gossip ...'

'Well?' The brown eyes met Fowler's in an open challenge.

'Had you any reason to believe or even to suspect that Riddle might have been the father of your daughter's baby?'

Jordan did not lose his temper or alter his tone of voice. 'The parentage of my grandson is no concern of the police, Mr Fowler.'

In view of his instructions Fowler decided to leave it at that. He picked his way along the muddy track to where he had left his car. The mist was clearing and he could see the sea. As he got into the car he heard a shout and saw Cissie running down the track towards him, disregarding the mud which splashed up over her legs as she ran. She was out of breath.

'Something to tell me?'

'No.' She held the car door open, hesitating what to say. 'I suppose you're here because you heard that Riddle was the father of my baby?'

'I'm here because my boss sent me.'

'Why else could they think that father was mixed up in this?'

Fowler shrugged. 'I don't know what they think, Miss, but I can guess.' He pointed to a corrugated iron shed three or four fields away. 'Isn't that where they found his clothes? That would be more than enough for them to take an interest.'

He could see that she was relieved. 'I never thought of it that way.'

'*Was* he the baby's father?'

'Of course not!'

'Who was?'

'I don't know. Haven't they told you I'm a bad lot?'

'You must have some idea.'

'If I have, I'm keeping it to myself.'

'Riddle's nephew – Matthew Choak?'

'Do me a favour!'

'We may have to ask you again.'

'No harm in asking.'

*   *   *

In telling his story to Wycliffe, Fowler added, 'There's something about that girl, sir. She's not just another trollop and she's obviously concerned about her father.'

'Is she intelligent?'

'Shrewd as they come.'

Wycliffe had been booked in at the one hotel which remained open through the year. It was perched on a small promontory to the east of the town, overlooking the bay. He was expecting to take his evening meal with five or six others in one corner of a dining-room designed to seat a hundred but, in fact, all the tables were occupied by delegates to some conference and he was asked to share with two of them. It was an all-male affair and each delegate wore a lettered, white disc pinned to his lapel which Wycliffe could not read. They were dressed in sober lounge suits and conversed in low voices, reminding him of a flock of rather dowdy sparrows pecking away at their food. He sat by a great semi-circular window which looked out into darkness pierced at regular intervals by the beam of the lighthouse. It surprised him that he was not drawn into conversation with the two at his table, but they evidently spoke only to their own. Perhaps the white disc was a necessary stimulus to articulation.

He would have been glad to talk, if only to escape the profitless treadmill of his thoughts – impressions rather than thoughts, random images which presented themselves again and again to his mind! The two women in the sombre, fusty dignity of the drawing-room at Buller's Hill House; Matthew Choak, trying his uncle's chair for size; the little room overlooking the bay where the undertaker kept his secret troubles locked up in a drawer like Pandora's box; the Scapegoat turning over and over in its garland of flame; the clothing, some of it blood-stained, spread out on tables in the police station.

He did not stay for coffee but left the hotel and walked down the almost deserted main street. The pavements were wet after recent rain. He turned off along one of the dimly-lit back streets and, making the most of his bump of direction, arrived at the foot of the steep slope which led up to *The Brigantine*, the pub where Tony had taken him.

The bar was comfortably full, but he saw no faces that he recognised. He bought his drink and found a seat next to a wizened little man in a seaman's jersey that was several sizes too big for him. The company was, as usual, subdued: Englishmen take their drinking seriously; but one little group near Wycliffe was more boisterous. The fun centred on a stocky individual with a flushed face and sandy hair. He had reached that stage of drunkenness in which he was astonished by his own cleverness and the others were egging him on.

'Look at that, then ... What you got to say about that?' He had pulled up the sleeve of his jersey, exposing a powerful arm covered with reddish hairs. He clenched his fist and exhibited his bulging biceps. 'You got to admit I'm a strong chap.'

'Yes, you're a strong chap, Ernie, no doubt about that.'

Ernie turned to one of the group. 'You just shake hands with me, Bert.'

Bert, a lanky, lugubrious individual, declined.

'Come on, Bert, I won't hurt you – straight up.'

Under pressure from the others Bert advanced a bony hand and Ernie took it in his massive fist. 'Now, jest tell me when I hurt.'

After a second Bert squealed and Ernie released him. 'See? And I was only playing.' He picked up his tankard and drank off half of it in one gulp. He wiped his mouth with the back of his hand and began to laugh. 'I done that once to the undertaker, only I didn't stop so soon, I squeezed him a bit harder ...' He seemed to derive pleasure from the memory. 'I used to work for the bugger – you know that, don't you?'

They agreed that they did.

'An' he give me the sack. "You come to my office and pick up your money an' your cards," he said. So I did. I was going to tell him what he could do with his job but I thought better of it an' I took my cards all polite like. Then I said, "No hard feelings, Mr Riddle," an' held out my hand to say goodbye like.' Ernie paused then added, 'They tol' me he was signing his letters with his left hand for a month afterwards.'

The story had a flattering reception.

'And now he's dead,' somebody said.

Ernie seemed to think about this. In the end he said, 'Oh, the bugger's dead all right but the question is, who's going to bury the undertaker?' He looked round, delighted with his sally. 'You get it? Who's going to bury the undertaker?' His eyes rested on Wycliffe and he leaned forward, touching Wycliffe on the knee. 'Who's going to bury the undertaker? That's what I want to know.'

Wycliffe looked at him, his face a mask of bland innocence. Ernie felt constrained to explain further. 'You don't understand, it's a riddle ... a *riddle*.' He broke off, enthralled by this new sample of his own wit, unconscious though it may have been, and everybody applauded.

'By God! You're on form tonight, Ernie. Good enough for the telly.'

But Ernie had suddenly become serious. Looking at Wycliffe, he said, 'I don't know you. I've never seen you before.'

'No, I don't think we've met.'

Ernie shook his head. 'I didn't like him – the undertaker, I mean; he was a bastard, he thought he was going to marry my wife.'

Ernie's companions seemed to think he'd gone far enough and were trying to distract his attention when a newcomer pushed his way into the group. He was sufficiently like Ernie to be a twin, but Wycliffe had the impression that he was younger as well as a good deal fitter. The newcomer spoke quietly. 'You've had enough, Ernie. Come on.'

Ernie's companions looked self-conscious. 'Don't be a spoil-sport, Sidney; Ernie's been telling us how he shook hands with the undertaker.'

But without a word, Ernie stood up and followed his brother unsteadily out of the bar, leaving a slightly embarrassed silence behind.

Wycliffe turned to his neighbour. 'Was that Sidney Passmore from the caravan site?'

The little man nodded. 'That's right, Sidney and his brother, Ernie. They look alike but they're as different as chalk and cheese.'

Chapter Five

WHEN HE CAME down to breakfast next morning Wycliffe found the hall full of suitcases; the conference was breaking up. Most of them had already breakfasted and he shared the dining-room with only a few others. This morning the sky was blue with powder-puff clouds and the sea sparkled so that he was dazzled when he looked at it. At home he rarely had more than a piece of toast and marmalade for breakfast, but when he was away he ate the whole cooked breakfast. It seemed the right thing to do, though he could not have said why.

He felt depressed despite the weather and he blamed the little seaside town, where life in the winter seemed to go on out of habit. He thought it a pity that the people could not hibernate like certain animals and come out again at Easter when they would once more have compelling and urgent business to attend to. The fact was that he was soured by a murder case with no body, by family enmity amounting to hatred, by a surfeit of gossip and a veneer of superstition which was much more than half pretence.

He reached his little office in the square, initialled a few reports, then asked for Sergeant Curtis. Curtis came in wearing a shabby, fawn mackintosh and looking exactly as he had done the night before. It was difficult to realise that he had been home, probably to a wife, perhaps to children, that he had slept, eaten and washed. Curtis was one of those rare souls who are born detective sergeants and have no thought of ever being anything else.

'We seem to have a surfeit of Passmores in this case, Curtis. I met the two brothers, Ernie and Sidney, last night.'

Curtis grinned. 'Ernie's a case; no wonder Laura divorced him.'

'What's he like? Just a sponger, or nasty with it?'

Curtis hesitated. 'I've never known him do anything vicious, though in drink he sometimes talks big. Usually he just takes the line of least resistance. As a matter of fact, despite everything, I think he was really fond of Laura and he certainly doted on the girl, Hilda.'

'He's been away, hasn't he?'

'That's right. He cleared off when Laura kicked him out, but he turned up again two or three weeks back, when his money ran out. At the moment he's living in one of brother Sidney's caravans.'

'About the caravans . . . this trouble over the fields, was that really serious for Sidney?'

Curtis raised his hands in a broad gesture. 'I'll say! That site is big business but Sidney's only got himself to blame. I ask you! All that investment dependent on somebody else's property!'

'What did Riddle want the land for?'

'God knows! Building eventually, I suppose. Anyway, he gave Sidney six months to quit.'

'Which didn't improve the Riddle image.'

Curtis laughed. 'The whole town pretended to be scandalised, but if the boot had been on the other foot – if Sidney, or anybody else for that matter, had done the same thing to Riddle – they would have had a good laugh and it would have been looked upon as good business.'

'You sound sorry for him.'

'In a way. He was a queer fish, but the town gave him a rough ride when they got the chance.'

The telephone rang and Wycliffe answered it. The coast-guards had spotted the Wheel off some rocks called The Idlers, about four miles down the coast.

Curtis was pleased. 'I thought they might, as soon as this fog lifted. You want it fetched in, sir?'

'I suppose so; how do we set about it?'

'Titch is our man. I saw his boat in the basin as I came along this morning. She was aground then, but there should be enough water to float her now.'

'Titch – a tall chap with a twisted lip?'

'That's him, sir, best seaman on the coast.'

Curtis telephoned the seamen's shelter and asked somebody to find Titch and get him to ring back.

'They'll find him, sir. Titch is never far away when there's money about.'

The call came through less than five minutes later and Curtis took it. 'Are you afloat, Titch? . . . The Wheel's been sighted off The Idlers . . . Yes, Mr Wycliffe wants you to fetch it in . . . Of course you'll be paid . . . No, somebody from here will go with you . . . Yes, I know there's wind coming up so the sooner the better . . . Okay, in fifteen minutes.'

Wycliffe decided to go with Curtis and to take with him his photographer, the dyspeptic Sergeant Smith, who protested that the motion of the boat would upset his stomach.

Titch was waiting on the quay with his launch berthed by the steps. He acknowledged Wycliffe with a twitch of the lips. Wycliffe and Curtis sat in the stern while Smith placed himself in the lee of the fo'c'sle on a little tip-up seat by the wheel. Titch produced yellow oilskins.

'You'll need these once we're outside the shelter of the point.'

In fact, they were no sooner through the harbour entrance than the launch began to throw up spray, surprising Wycliffe, who had thought how peaceful the sea looked in the morning sun. Titch steered close in to the point and Wycliffe could see the broad path of the Wheel and the mound of turves by which it had been shot into the air before its final plunge into the sea. The spray was coming inboard now; Wycliffe and Curtis pulled their oilskins round them, and Smith crouched on his perch, his grey moustache glistening with droplets of moisture. Ahead a ragged coastline stretched away to a long, low headland which jutted out into the sea, its level surface broken by the jagged stumps of two mine stacks.

Curtis pointed: 'Grumbla Head. The Idlers lie in the lee of the head, close to the shoreline.'

The waves had white caps now and they seemed to effervesce

as they swept by. Every now and then the launch took a larger wave on her starboard bow and she would shy away like a frightened colt. Wycliffe, none too happy himself, felt a pang of remorse as he watched Smith who, pale, with a set expression, sat clutching with one hand at a stay of the stumpy mast and holding on to his seat with the other.

Slowly they began to feel the protection of Grumbla Head and within half-an-hour they had entered relatively calm water. They were making for the angle between the shore and the base of the headland and as they approached Wycliffe could see tall, black rocks rising out of the sea like the truncated and eroded pillars of some giant temple. At first they seemed so close together as to form an impassable barrier, but as they drew nearer it became clear that they were several yards apart.

'The Idlers,' Curtis said.

Titch had cut back the motor and was scanning the shoreline. Suddenly he pointed. 'There she is.'

He seemed to be pointing into the middle of The Idlers, and Wycliffe watched with uneasy fascination as he brought the launch between two of the rocks. They now seemed enormous, with the swell surging up their black, shining sides. The engine was just ticking over and the launch seemed to nose into the maze as though feeling her own way. Despite the swell the water was smooth and dark and oily, with great masses of weed which rose and fell in a slow rhythm.

'There,' Curtis pointed.

Wycliffe saw a gull which seemed to be standing on the water but as he watched it took off with a derisive squawk and he caught sight of the lattice framework of the Wheel lifting to the swell. Titch cruised past the Wheel, then put the motor astern and backed up to it. Within a foot of the Wheel he went momentarily ahead, then knocked the motor out. The launch held her place, riding the swell as though held to the Wheel by invisible ties.

'We'd better have a photograph.'

However bad he felt, Smith took a couple of shots. They could see the outline of the Wheel plainly enough now, floating just level with the surface of the water, draped with clinging weeds.

'We'll tow on a short line,' Titch said. He reached over the stern and lifted the Wheel until the lower rim rested on the transom to one side of the stern post. Most of the framework of the Wheel was now visible; scorched and blackened branches of yew and laurel were still entangled with the osiers along with the seaweeds, but there was no sign of the Scapegoat.

Wycliffe tried to concentrate on the Wheel and to ignore the veritable forest of giant rock pinnacles with which they were surrounded. It concerned him the more to see that Titch, also, appeared to have no eyes for anything but the Wheel. The launch, however, behaved like a well-trained work-horse and merely rose and fell with the swell.

The Wheel was made fast, resting on the transom and trailing in the water. Titch knocked the engine in and they began to draw slowly away. As they passed between the two pillars along the path by which they had entered, the Wheel cleared with plenty of room to spare.

Curtis said, 'We shall take longer getting back because of the drag, but it won't be so choppy with the wind behind us. We'll go for'ard; if we catch a stern sea we shan't want that thing round our necks.' So they sat on the engine housing and Wycliffe felt sufficiently relaxed to light his pipe.

By the time they entered the harbour it was high tide and the launch, with the Wheel riding her stern, lay almost level with the quay. It was none too soon; smoke-grey clouds scurried across the sky and even in the harbour the wind was whipping up little white-topped waves.

Titch spoke out of the side of his mouth. 'We timed that nice; the blow's just beginning.'

Quite a crowd of people had gathered on the quay, but they were well behaved and they allowed ample room for the Wheel to be dragged ashore and stood on its rims. For the first time Wycliffe was able to examine the details of its construction. There was no hub and there were no spokes; in fact, the whole of the centre of the Wheel was clear of any obstruction. It consisted of two concentric structures, the outer one nine feet and the inner one six feet in diameter. The Scapegoat had been secured by 'wrists' and 'ankles' to the inner ring and Wycliffe thought he could make out the four points where the ropes had been. To his surprise he noticed that they seemed to have burned into the wood.

Curtis said that the Wheel could be accommodated in a shed in the police station yard, so Wycliffe left him to organise transport. The crowd of bystanders made way for him and he caught sight of Ernie Passmore among them. He was talking to a young girl with straight, fair hair and they were both very serious. Wycliffe wondered if the fair girl was his daughter.

He wanted to settle, once and for all, the question of whether Riddle had made his last journey inside the Wheel and for that reason he was resolved to have it closely examined by an expert. He telephoned the Forensic Science Laboratory and arranged for someone to be sent down. There were a number of reports on his desk, almost all of them negative, including one from the officer in charge of the search around Jordan's farm. They had covered an area averaging a quarter of a mile across and extending a mile beyond the farm, along the cliffs, with no result. Wycliffe decided to call off the search which would release at least a dozen men to return to normal duties.

It was late in the afternoon when he realised that he had eaten nothing since breakfast, and he was about to go out into the town in search of a restaurant when the telephone rang. It was Zelah.

'Charles! Why on earth didn't you tell us? ... I had no idea until I heard it quite by chance ... You must get out of that hotel and come and stay with us ... Of course you must ... But that is quite absurd ... My dear man, what sort of people do you think we are? Can you imagine poor old Tony and me conspiring to deflect the course of justice? ... Well, you may be right at that ... All right, if you insist, but do come round this evening and give us another chance to try to persuade you ... Yes, for a meal, this time *I* insist.'

Of course he had to go, but he promised himself, 'Just this once.'

When he left the hall to go to his hotel he was surprised by the wind. As he came out of the shelter of the square into the main street he was caught unawares and almost swept off his feet. It occurred to him that the small squares and staggered alleys might have a practical as well as an aesthetic function. From his hotel bedroom the sea was a great waste of dirty grey flecked with white, the clouds were ragged and seemed to race across the sky and, as he watched, a great fountain of spray shot up from the base of the little promontory on which the hotel was built. It was getting dark, but there was no trace of a sunset.

After a bath and a leisurely drink at the public bar he took his car and drove up the hill on to the moor. It was dark and the car was buffeted by the wind; the headlights were scarcely reflected from the black road surface or from the moorland turf on either side. The road at that point was half-a-mile inland from the cliffs and Jordan's place lay between it and the sea on what the geologists call an elevated plain of marine denudation. On the other side of the road, to Wycliffe's left, the ground rose fairly steeply, and it was on this slope, covered with gorse and heather and strewn with huge boulders, that the Ballards had their home.

He was concerned that he might miss the turning, but fresh granite chippings gleamed white in his headlights and he turned off, ruefully aware of the wear and tear on his tyres, to say nothing of the suspension. The drive snaked across the flank of the hill to a levelled clearing which had once been the site of a mine; a giant stack still stood within a hundred yards of their door.

As he entered the paved courtyard the rain came whipping in from the sea, lashing against the car and obliterating everything. They must have seen his lights for they were at the door, and a couple of minutes later he was in their brightly-lit living-room standing by a blazing fire and being asked what he would drink.

It was very pleasant after all.

Zelah was a good cook and he enjoyed the meal. The granite-built house nestled into the hillside as though part of it and the gale roared overhead. Soon one could ignore it, except now and then when the fire seemed to take a huge breath and glowed with

87

a sudden fierceness which sent sparks flying crazily up the chimney.

They talked of Zelah's forthcoming debut on television and of Tony's plans for a spring exhibition at a London gallery. They were tactful in avoiding any reference to the case and it was Wycliffe who, mellowed by good food and a couple of glasses of Burgundy, brought it up.

'We picked up the Wheel this afternoon.'

'Yes, we heard. That was when we found out you were down.' Zelah was clearing the table.

'Picked it up off The Idlers.' Wycliffe tried to sound casual as though these nautical exercises were everyday events.

'No Scapegoat, human or otherwise?'

'No.'

Zelah had taken out one tray of dishes and was returning for a second. 'It's puzzled me for years that four times out of five the Wheel is recovered, but I can't recollect a single instance of the Scapegoat being brought in.'

Tony was in the kitchen making coffee but the door was open. 'Surely the whole object of the exercise is to get rid of the Scapegoat.'

Zelah was patient, as with a child. 'I know that, darling, but one wonders how it happens with such unfailing regularity.'

Tony came in with the coffee.

'Jordan is a cunning old rogue.'

'But what can he *do*?'

'Have you ever looked at the design of the Wheel – before it's been dressed up?'

'I did, this afternoon,' Wycliffe said. 'I was struck by the fact that there were no spokes, the whole centre is open.'

Tony started pouring coffee.

'Exactly. When the Wheel hits the water it floats on its side. If there were spokes and the Scapegoat happened to be topside of them it couldn't fall through.'

'But it must be tied in any case.'

'Yes, to the circumference of the inner wheel.'

'Well, then?'

'He uses binder twine, but plaited in with the twine is a slow-burning fuse.'

'You've never told me all this!' Zelah was accusing.

'You've never asked me, dear. I thought you preferred not to know about the mechanics of miracles.'

'But how do you know?'

'That would be telling.'

'Pig!'

'Surely the Scapegoat, even if it broke free, would float.' Wycliffe was interested.

'It would if he didn't put a quarter-hundredweight of scrap iron inside it.'

Zelah was shocked. 'You mean that the whole thing is a fraud?'

'Well, you didn't really suppose that he was cleansing our little community of its sin?'

'Well, no, of course not, but it's so blatant.'

'It isn't blatant if you don't know about it. You can't blame him. His little show wouldn't stand much chance of survival if it even hinted at a bad "season" to come. In any case, he's almost certainly no more devious than his Celtic predecessors in the job.'

For once, Zelah could think of nothing to say.

Wycliffe sipped his coffee, which was just to his liking, and stretched his legs to the fire in a mood of expansive goodwill.

'One of the many things I don't understand is why Riddle was so generally disliked, even hated. He seems to have been a pretty hard-headed business man, but there must be plenty of others in a town of this size . . .'

'Jealousy,' Zelah said.

For once Tony contradicted his wife. 'There's more to it than that. Charles is right; there are others in the town who have done well for themselves, sometimes by methods less creditable than the undertaker's, and they're highly thought of. Riddle suffered for being the boy in the corner of the playground.'

Zelah looked at him in amused astonishment. 'What *are* you talking about, Tony?'

'I mean that he was always the odd one out. His looks, his

temperament, his background – even his name marked him off for ridicule. I ask you – Johnny Riddle! His father was a Seventh Day Adventist and used to go round the streets carrying a placard with "Prepare to meet thy God" on one side and "Sin is Death" on the other.'

Zelah chuckled. 'I'd forgotten. We used to call him Jehovah Johnny.'

'Exactly. In my experience people will forgive a lot of things, but not being beaten at their own game by someone they've always looked upon as a caricature.'

Wycliffe stayed chatting until after midnight and had to drive back in conditions which were, if anything, worse than they had been earlier. It was not raining, but at times it seemed that the car would be lifted off the road. All the same he felt that he must look in at the hall before going to his hotel.

The little square was relatively sheltered, and in the hall the gale was no more than a distant, muffled roar. A detective constable was dozing by the telephone, his feet on the table.

'All quiet?'

The constable sprang to his feet. 'Sorry, sir, I didn't hear you come in.'

'Anything happening?'

'Nothing, sir. Mr Scales looked in earlier.'

'Goodnight.'

Wycliffe went back to his hotel and to bed.

Chapter Six

ON FRIDAY MORNING the gale was as fierce as ever and during the night the high tide had flooded the shops on the waterfront. People were busy sweeping out and council workmen had brought sandbags as a defence against a possible repeat performance by the afternoon tide. The tumbled surface of the sea looked blue-green, with white horses as far as the eye could see.

Wycliffe found Sergeant Curtis sitting at a table in the hall, typing yet another report. It was a wonder that with his huge fingers he managed to avoid striking two keys at once. Wycliffe perched himself on the edge of the table.

'Do you know Laura Passmore's daughter – Hilda, isn't it?'

Curtis's tiny eyes, ludicrously close together, registered mild surprise. 'Hilda? Yes, I know her. Nice kid; sixteen or thereabouts. Since she left school she's been working for the Fish Co-operative in Stockholm Backs, not far from Riddle's yard.' He studied his outspread hands as though surprised to see them, then went on: 'She's going round with Sidney's boy – Ralph.'

'Her cousin?'

Curtis nodded. 'You're catching on, sir. I don't think her choice pleases her mother.'

'Is he a decent lad?'

'Seems so. Clever with it. He's in the sixth form, working for his A-levels, and they reckon he might go to Oxford.' Curtis shrugged. 'I don't know where he gets it from; certainly not from poor old Sidney.'

Wycliffe slid off the table and wandered away into his little office. Curtis looked after him with an understanding grin; the two men had a lot in common.

'It's not easy to dispose of a body.'

Wycliffe did not say the words aloud but his lips formed them. That was the way his mind worked; he would be struck by a sentence or a phrase, then he would worry at it, turning it this way and that.

Riddle was tall and big-boned; a heavy man. To dispose of his corpse would be difficult . . .

Matthew Choak, Timothy Jordan, Sidney Passmore and his brother, Ernie, Riddle's mother and his sister, Sarah, Laura Passmore and her daughter, Hilda. Now, Sidney's son, Ralph.

These were the people whose paths had crossed Riddle's, those whose lives would be affected one way or another by the difference between Riddle living and Riddle dead. Wycliffe's detectives were already gathering information about most of them.

'Collect and collate' had been the maxim of Wycliffe's former chief. Wycliffe had no maxims, but that was exactly what was being done, though to him it seemed of paramount importance to build a clear picture of the victim himself.

A murder victim is not a stage-prop in the drama of his death but an active participant. Even if he is murdered by a homicidal maniac he has chosen to be at a certain place at a certain time. But most killers are not homicidal maniacs and the victim contributes much more than a mere coincidence of time and place to his own fate. Riddle had been murdered, so which of his actions, accomplished or intended, had prompted his killing?

The more he thought of it the more he was inclined to the idea that the murderer lacked any single, clearly defined motive. Perhaps he or she found justification in a seemingly intolerable accumulation of slights, insults and deprivations . . .

Sergeant Bourne came in and hovered until Wycliffe spoke to him.

'Two things, sir. Forensic rang to say that a Mr Horton is on his way, and Matthew Choak is waiting to see you. He refuses to talk to anybody else.'

'All right, bring him up.'

An area at the far end of the hall had been screened off as a waiting-room and now Bourne escorted Matthew between the double row of tables, most of them empty. He looked like death; there were dark rings under his eyes and the pale skin was drawn tightly over his cheekbones.

'I thought you were going with your mother to see Mr Penver this morning?'

Matthew sat in the chair opposite Wycliffe.

'Mother wanted me to, but what good would it do? It wouldn't alter my uncle's will. In any case, it came as no surprise to me.'

'Does that mean that you knew the contents of your uncle's will before your mother told you?' Matthew did not answer at once and Wycliffe went on: 'When I spoke to you last you told me that you knew nothing of his intentions.'

Matthew was looking at the floor and did not raise his eyes. 'That was true, really. I didn't know any details, but a month or so ago I had a row with my uncle and he said then that I mustn't count on anything from him; if I did I'd be disappointed.'

'Did you believe him?'

'He never said anything he didn't mean.'

'What was the row about?'

Matthew's hands were gripped tightly between his knees. 'Just a difference of opinion about a job.'

'When you went to see Mr Penver about the day-to-day running of the business, what did he tell you?'

'That he'd arranged for the bank to cash cheques on his and my signature until all this is settled.'

Wycliffe looked at the young man and wondered how much longer he could carry on. A nervous tremor affected his lower lip and he looked as though at any moment he might burst into tears.

'Mr Choak, why did you come here this morning?'

He looked up and, for once, met Wycliffe's eyes. 'To tell you what Penver had arranged about the business; you said you wanted to know.'

'You are sure that you have nothing else to tell me?'

'No, nothing. How could I?'

He was dealing with a congenital liar, but was he dealing with a murderer?

'Is your car all right now?'

Matthew shrugged. 'As right as it will ever be. I went out there next day with a friend from a garage and he got it going; it was grit in the carburettor.'

'That night you walked home, did you meet anyone?'

'I told you, two or three cars passed me but they didn't stop.'

'Does your mother drive?'

He looked mildly surprised by the question. 'Mother? She hardly knows one end of a car from the other. If she wants to go anywhere I take her or she goes with uncle.'

Wycliffe was asking questions almost at random, trying to stimulate some animation but Matthew sat there like a well-trained dog, ready to make a given response at the appropriate signal. Wycliffe let him go.

Before going out Wycliffe again studied the map and got Curtis to point out places in which he was interested.

'The Fish Co-operative is here, just a few steps from Riddle's yard. Sidney lives out here on the eastern side of the town where the fish cellars used to be. They call it The Linny, and Sidney lives in one of the big new houses. His caravan site is a quarter of a mile up the valley from his house at a place called Miller's Bottom – here, it's marked.

'Laura's house is in Salvation Street, backing on the headland. Here's the street, right at the far end of the harbour.'

Wycliffe walked the length of the waterfront to where the road petered out in a footpath to the headland. Salvation Street was on his left, a double row of cottages which cut across the low neck of land. The wind showed no signs of abating, but the tide was out and the inner basin was an expanse of fine, yellow sand. Even so, the air was full of spray and every now and then a drift of spume, like soap suds, whipped past on the wind. He turned down Salvation Street and gained some shelter from the houses, which were small, granite-built, with their front doors opening on the street. In most of the windows the curtains were partly drawn so that the rooms must have been dark, but the people probably lived in the back. He saw nobody.

Number sixteen, where Laura lived, was at the far end. He knocked on the green-painted door and after a brief interval it was opened.

'Mrs Passmore?'

She was fair, well covered but not fat, and good looking except for hard lines round her mouth. There was an agreeable smell of cooking.

'What do you want?'

Wycliffe introduced himself.

'You'd better come in.'

She hesitated by the door of the sitting-room, then walked on down the passage. 'It'll have to be the kitchen because of the baby.'

The kitchen was bigger than he had supposed; it had a stone floor with a large square of matting, an open grate and a tiny window looking out on the rising ground of the headland. A door led into a scullery where he could see a sink and a gas cooker on which a saucepan puffed little jets of steam. An old lady sat by the fire in an armchair of slatted wood and a little boy was pushing a toy lorry on the mat.

'My mother.'

The old lady acknowledged him with a nod. Laura went to the scuttle and shovelled coal on the fire.

'You don't have to beat about the bush; you've come about Mr Riddle. I could say that you've come to the wrong place, but I won't.'

'The wrong place?'

'You should be talking to them, asking them questions.'

'Them?'

She looked at him with suspicion. 'His mother, his sister and most of all that precious nephew.'

The old lady was looking anxious; she belonged to a generation and a class more easily impressed by policemen. 'Laura, there's no call–'

'You keep out of this, mother. It's no concern of yours.' She poked the fire with unnecessary violence.

'I understand that you were to marry Mr Riddle?'

'That's right, early in the new year, it was all fixed. Now . . .' She broke off and her glance round the bare kitchen was more eloquent than words.

'I'm sorry.'

The little boy slipped, fell on his lorry and whimpered for a while. She comforted him with lavish endearments before turning back to Wycliffe.

'They were all against it.'

'You mean his family?'

'Everybody. You could understand it with his family – more or less; they had something to lose, or thought they had.'

Wycliffe was seated on a kitchen chair by the large, square table covered with a plastic cloth.

'I don't want to upset you, Mrs Passmore, but it looks as though Mr Riddle was murdered and it is my job to find who killed him.'

'And I hope you do. My God, I hope you do!'

She was off into the scullery to stir the stew; she was one of those women who will never give anybody the satisfaction of her undivided attention.

'Did you see Mr Riddle on Friday evening?'

'Friday?'

'The evening he disappeared.'

'No, I was in all the evening and he certainly didn't come here.'

'He was last seen walking along Albert Terrace in the direction of the hill down to Moorgate. Can you suggest where he might have been going?'

She looked vaguely surprised. 'No, I can't. I've no idea.'

'I imagine you knew him pretty well.'

She looked at him sharply, then away again. 'We were getting to know each other.'

'He confided in you?'

'Some things; more as time went on. He had nobody to talk to, he needed companionship. And so do I. That's what it was all about.'

The little boy had gone over to his granny because his nose was running. His mother saw him and dashed upstairs. 'I'll get a handkerchief.'

While she was gone the old lady looked across at Wycliffe. 'It's not easy for her – divorced, with a young child.'

'No.'

'All the same, she's well out of that tangle with the undertaker. I never shed no tears when I heard he was most likely dead.'

Laura came down with a handkerchief and wiped her son's nose.

'They all had it in for Jonathan and they did what they could to harm him, but they were glad enough of his money, of his custom in their shops and of the work he provided.'

'Did Mr Riddle tell you anything which suggested that he was on particularly bad terms with anybody? Did he speak of a recent row or of serious friction with anyone?'

She carried the little boy back to his lorry and set him down. 'There now! Harold play with his lorry; there's a good boy!'

'I suppose you mean about Matthew; he told me that.'

'What did he tell you?'

She looked surprised. 'I suppose you've talked to Mr Bryant?'

'Mr Bryant?'

'Bryant and Sons, the builders' merchants. Matthew and one of Bryant's clerks were fiddling the invoices; they swindled Jonathan out of more than eight hundred pounds and Jonathan found out. Mr Bryant sacked the clerk but Jonathan kept Matthew on and told him he would have to pay all the money back out of his wages, so much a month.'

The old lady was agog. 'You never told me that! Not that I'm surprised; they're all tarred with the same brush, that family; the boy's no better and no worse than his mother or his uncle. I remember when Sarah Riddle was no more than a schoolgirl she was had up for ...'

'Mother! You've no right to talk like that. I've told you, this is none of your business.'

'When did Mr Riddle discover the fraud?'

She shrugged. 'A month or six weeks ago.'

No wonder Matthew had been like a man awaiting sentence. He must have known that it was bound to come out, and when it did his case would appear that much blacker. Perhaps he had been trying to pluck up courage to tell Wycliffe himself.

'I felt sure Mr Bryant would have been in touch when he heard about Jonathan.'

97

Wycliffe said nothing. A squall of rain hit the little window with a noise like hailstones and found its way down the chimney, hissing on the coals.

'Did Mr Riddle come here often?'

'He's been here a few times.'

'When he was here, did he make himself at home?'

She gave him a suspicious look. 'What are you getting at?'

'I'm asking you if he relaxed when he was here. Did he behave like a guest or did he take his jacket off and sit in front of the fire like one of the family?'

'He made himself at home. There was no reason why he shouldn't.'

'Of course not.' Wycliffe wanted her to talk, not merely to answer questions, and he tried to give her a new lead. 'He doesn't seem to have been well-liked.'

She sniffed. 'Jealousy. They were jealous of his success, they spread rumours about him – lies. It was wicked!'

'Some people are saying that his body was substituted for the Scapegoat on Saturday night.'

He was surprised to see that she had lost colour. For the first time she sat down and gave him her whole attention. 'I know what they're saying, but you don't think it could have happened, do you?' Her manner was strangely tense.

Wycliffe was cautious. 'On the face of it, it seems unlikely, but I suppose it's possible.'

She nodded. 'I keep telling myself that it *isn't* possible, that I imagined it.'

'Hadn't you better tell me?'

She hesitated, looking at her mother, who was hanging on every word, then at Wycliffe. 'All right, for what it's worth. The last time I saw Jonathan was Thursday evening when he picked me up in the car and we went for a drive. Now that my divorce has come through we thought it was time to tell people that we were getting married and start seeing each other openly. He was going to tell his mother and sister on the Friday and, to break the ice, we decided to go to the Fire Festival on Saturday; he was to pick me up here at eight and we were going together.'

She broke off and sat for a moment staring in the fire. When she resumed her voice was unsteady. 'He didn't turn up. I waited for half-an-hour or so, then I went out to the phone box on the quay and rang his home. Sarah answered. She was about as friendly as you'd expect, but she told me he wasn't home. When I started to ask questions she just hung up.'

'What did you do?'

'I began to wonder whether I'd made a mistake over the arrangement. I told myself he might have meant us to meet at the Festival, so I went along there and searched for him in the crowd.' Her voice almost let her down but she persevered. 'You can't understand. I thought he must have stood me up ... backed out at the last minute . . . I thought this might be his way of telling me.'

She gave herself time to regain her self-control and when she spoke again her manner was more composed.

'I admit I was getting into a state. I could see myself losing everything . . .' She looked round the kitchen, at the child and at her mother. 'Then I ran into Matthew and I asked him if he'd seen his uncle. Matthew, as usual, was unwilling to answer a straight question, but I got it out of him in the end. He hadn't seen his uncle since Friday and they had no idea where he was.'

'Did you believe him?'

'I didn't know what to believe, I'd got so worked up . . .' The little boy, sensing that his mother was upset, had come to stand by her and she lifted him on to her lap. 'It was then that they released the Wheel and it came bowling down the hill not more than ten yards from where I was standing. As I looked, the mask of the Scapegoat caught fire and curled up . . .' She stopped speaking.

Wycliffe did not prompt her but her mother, evidently hearing all this for the first time, had no such scruples. 'Well?'

'I don't know. For an instant I thought I saw his face behind the mask – it was only an instant and then it was gone, but I nearly fainted. Then I told myself that it was the state I was in and somehow I pulled myself together and came home.'

Wycliffe sat silently; even the old lady seemed to feel that too ready speech would be out of place. In the end it was Laura who broke the silence.

'First thing Sunday morning I rang his home again and spoke to Sarah. I asked her if he'd returned home and she told me to mind my own business. In the end I went to the police and found that she'd just reported that he was missing.'

Wycliffe nodded. 'All I can say is that when we brought in the Wheel yesterday there was no sign of the Scapegoat.'

'You think it's possible that he was . . . ?'

'I think it very unlikely.'

She seemed reassured.

Wycliffe tried again. 'Mrs Passmore, I don't want to add to your distress but I have to ask you whether, in your opinion, it is likely that Mr Riddle had relations with other women or with one other woman?'

He was surprised by her response, 'I've no idea but I shouldn't wonder at it.' She glanced at her mother, then went on, 'Jonathan needed companionship – he was a lonely man – but I don't think sex was very important to him.'

Wycliffe thanked her for being so frank and got up to leave. She came to the door with him, hugging herself against the wind, and her manner was almost friendly.

At the end of the street he had the option of turning left, into the town, or right, along the road which skirted the shore and led to Moorgate and the hill to Albert Terrace. The rain had stopped and he turned right. The road, which was narrow, was separated from a low cliff by a stretch of rough grass. The cliff sloped to a rocky shore where breakers thundered against the ledges about three hundred yards from where he was. With each wave spray shot scores of feet into the air and was caught by the wind and whisked inland. There were no houses in sight; the sea on one side and steeply rising ground on the other had so far discouraged developers. Then, as he turned a corner, he came upon a little house, level with the road, built on concrete stilts above the rocks. It was painted pink and surrounded by white, wooden palings so that it looked like an overgrown doll's house. There was a wooden porch over the front door, elaborately carved, and canopies over the windows of similar design. Presumably the folly of some eccentric before the days of planning.

He stopped to look at the house and saw below it, on the shore, a large rectangular basin which seemed to have been blasted out of the rock at the foot of the cliff. Now, at half-tide, with the sea driven by a gale, the bottom of the basin was covered with shallow, turbulent water. A hundred yards or so beyond the house there were steps down to the shore and, curious, he went down to look more closely. His first impression was that somebody had started to construct a small harbour, but then he saw a shallow groove cut in the face of the cliff which must at one time have accommodated a pipe, and it occurred to him that it had probably been a sewage outfall.

He stood on the edge of the basin and, although it was not raining, his mackintosh was wet with spray and water trickled down his forehead and cheeks. He looked up at the house and through a dormer window he could make out the outline of a figure, seated and immobile, facing the sea.

At the level he now was the breakers looked menacing, as though at any moment they might sweep in to engulf him. He climbed back up to the road and walked on. Around the next corner he came to a hairpin bend where the road turned abruptly inland and up hill to Albert Terrace. A kissing-gate led to the moor and beyond it the path climbed steeply.

He turned back.

It was still possible that the undertaker had been visiting Laura Passmore on the evening he disappeared, but why go to her by such a roundabout way? Their association was no longer to be kept secret and, anyway, Laura denied that he had come.

As he came once more in sight of the queer little house on stilts, he saw a woman in a shiny red mackintosh and waterproof hat to match, opening the garden gate. She was carrying a shopping bag and had evidently just returned from town.

'Good morning. Rough, isn't it?'

She laughed. 'I'm used to it.'

A girl in her late twenties, a fat girl with a mop of hair which refused to be confined within her hat.

'I've been admiring your little house.'

She glanced up at the house. 'It's got its attractions, but you should have been in it last night.'

'I wondered how it came to be built here.'

'The council built it, way back. It was for the man who looked after the sewage outfall; he had to be here to open the sluice whenever the tide was right. Father had the job, but when they built the new outfall on the other side of town we stayed on here. In fact, father bought the place. He's retired now and crippled with arthritis – hardly ever moves out of his room.'

'I'm sorry.'

'Well, it comes to all of us one way or another.' She grinned. 'At least, that's what they say.' She looked him up and down. 'Are you on holiday?'

'No, I'm a detective enquiring into the disappearance of Jonathan Riddle.'

'I thought you might be. I've had one of your chaps round already, asking whether I saw him go by that evening.'

'And did you?'

'In the dark?' She laughed. She had charm, a way of making you feel that you were joining her in some harmless conspiracy.

'You knew him?'

'Oh, I knew him all right. Everybody knew the undertaker.'

Wycliffe walked on towards the town, but he avoided the waterfront and returned instead by the main street, which was narrow enough to give some shelter from the gale. Housewives were out shopping and he saw Sarah, a scarf over her head, wearing an old grey top-coat, carrying a shopping bag in one hand and clutching a large, black handbag with brass fastenings in the other. She looked at him and her lips moved, but nothing audible came from them.

Horton, from the forensic laboratory, had arrived. He was a man in his forties, quiet and unassuming. He brought laboratory reports on the undertaker's clothing and other items which had been sent to him and he had already spent an hour examining the Wheel.

'I've taken scrapings of those areas where the Scapegoat appears to have been secured to the frame. We should be able to tell you something of the nature of the fastenings used but I doubt if we can say whether a body was involved. Mr Bourne mentioned a fuse incorporated in plaited binder-twine; this would explain the deep scorch marks. If there was a body, it's possible that the singeing of skin and flesh might have left identifiable organic deposits on the woodwork, but the Wheel has been in the water for some time and we mustn't expect much.'

Mr Horton's voice and manner were soothing. One could imagine him in the witness box, speaking in a dull monotone, taking his time to answer counsel's questions and giving clear, unshakable explanations or admitting his ignorance plainly. It would be difficult to dramatise Horton into a laboratory wizard on whom a man's freedom might depend.

'As far as the clothing is concerned, it's all in the reports, but to save you time I can tell you more or less what we found and it isn't a great deal. The blood is human and belongs to group A and to group M on the Landsteiner-Levine system. It is rhesus positive. Our haematologist is of the opinion that the blood was derived from a fresh wound in contact, or almost in contact, with the material of the shirt collar.

'There are indications of scorching and the presence of particles of smokeless powder suggest a firearm wound, the weapon having been discharged at close range.'

Horton broke off and looked at Wycliffe as though apologising for boring him.

'There was a certain amount of dandruff on the shirt collar and more on the collar of the jacket. We removed human hairs from several items of clothing and they fall into three categories. Black, rather coarse, straight hairs are most plentiful; then there were finer, dark-brown hairs on the jacket and shirt; finally, we picked up a few animal hairs almost certainly from a cat.'

Wycliffe felt stolid and dull; he listened with only half an ear and his thoughts wandered.

'The brown hairs show signs of artificial waving and this, coupled with their fineness, suggests a woman, though such evidence is by no means conclusive.'

Laura Passmore had fair hair, Riddle's sister was grey and his mother white. The old lady had said, 'I told you, there's a woman.'

'I'm sorry that we weren't able to do more ...'

Wycliffe felt like patting him on the head, but he thanked him and saw him off with his samples, then he went back to his little office and sat staring at the wall.

It was less than seventy-two hours since he had heard of the finding of Riddle's clothes, but it seemed much longer. He had not yet met all the people concerned; too many of them were still only names.

A large spider's web occupied one corner of the room near the ceiling and he could just make out the spider lurking there, quite motionless; emulating Mr Micawber, waiting for something to turn up. Wycliffe was well aware that large numbers of people spend their lives studying spiders and insects, centipedes and millipedes ... They catch them and pickle them or pin them on cards; they put them in various sorts of cages and study their responses to different environments and different stimuli ... Experiments under controlled conditions ... Cutting down the number of variables. In that respect, he envied them; he worked with human beings, on whom all studies have to be done in the wild.

There was a knock on the door and Scales came in. Perhaps the glassy stare had lingered in his eyes, for Scales looked at him queerly. Wycliffe waved him to a seat.

They chatted for a while, bringing each other up to date.

Scales said, 'It looks bad for young Choak; in his case there's a double motive, the money which he stole and has to pay back and what he could reasonably have expected under his uncle's will.'

'But he says that he expected nothing.'

'That wasn't what he said before.'

Wycliffe agreed vaguely. He was not really thinking about Matthew Choak but about the dead man.

'I keep coming back to the same point, John. If we are to believe the evidence of the bloodstains, Riddle was in his shirt sleeves when he was killed: no jacket, no outer coat ...'

'You think that's important, sir?' Scales was cautious.

'Don't you? As far as we know there were only two places where he was likely to feel sufficiently at home to take his jacket off – in his own house and at Laura Passmore's.'

Scales opened his mouth to say something but changed his mind. Wycliffe stood up.

'I'm going to have a word with Laura's daughter, Hilda.'

In her letter, which Wycliffe had found in the undertaker's desk, Hilda had said that she was alone in the office from twelve to one each day and it was now half-past twelve.

Because of the wind and the frequent squalls of rain there were few people about, but he was aware of being watched. They watched him with interest, but also with suspicion, even apprehension; no one knows what an official snooper on the loose will turn up.

To get to the Fish Co-operative he had to pass Riddle's yard and as he did so Matthew was getting into one of the firm's vans; he carried a clip-board and a surveying tape. He saw Wycliffe and acknowledged him with a timid gesture.

The Co-operative also had double doors with a wicket gate leading into a cobbled yard. Two lorries were parked in the yard, which was littered with piles of boxes stinking of fish. A flight of granite steps to his right led to the first floor of one of the buildings and an arrow carried the word, 'Office'.

He did not move quietly by intention, but as he pushed upon the door of the office a boy and girl sprang apart. They were both flushed and embarrassed.

'Miss Passmore?'

She was plain, with long, straight hair, but her features were good and one day, soon, she would undergo that magical transformation into a beautiful woman.

'My name is Wycliffe; I heard that you were on your own here between twelve and one.'

If the shot found its mark she gave no sign. She said, simply, 'I know who you are.'

'I suppose this is Ralph?'

The boy nodded.

'Not at school?'

'It's half-term.'

Wycliffe's manner was relaxed and friendly, but they were wary.

'I really came for a word with Miss Passmore, but if she doesn't mind you hearing what I have to say ...'

The girl indicated by a barely perceptible gesture that she was indifferent.

The room, warmed by a large oil-stove, was close; a window with tiny panes looked out over slate roofs to a distant, misty sea.

Wycliffe took her letter to Riddle from his pocket and laid it on the desk in front of her. She glanced at it but said nothing.

'Why did you ask Mr Riddle to meet you?'

'I wanted to talk to him.'

'What about?'

'He was going to marry my mother.'

'And you wanted to persuade him out of it?'

A tiny hesitation. 'Yes.'

'Anything else?'

She glanced across at Ralph, who continued to look acutely uncomfortable. 'I wanted to ask him to be more reasonable with my uncle over the fields.'

Wycliffe had perched himself on a stool between Hilda, who was seated at her desk, and Ralph, who sat on a seat like a chapel pew.

'Your uncle, Ralph's father, is that right?'

She flushed slightly. 'Yes.'

'What were you offering as an inducement?'

'I don't understand what you mean.'

'Mr Riddle has a reputation for being a good business man, even a hard man; did you think you stood any chance of persuading him out of two important objectives without offering anything in return?'

'It was worth trying.'

'Did he come?'

'Yes, Thursday lunchtime.'

'What did he say?'

'That he would think it over.'

'What was he like? Was he polite, bantering or aggressive?'

'He was polite, why shouldn't he be?'

Wycliffe realised that she was astute, but she puzzled him. He was sure that the girl had something to hide, something that was embarrassing rather than incriminating, but he could not imagine what it was. Was it possible that she had tried to bribe the undertaker with her body? It seemed unlikely, but Wycliffe knew from long experience that what young people may do in certain circumstances, especially where loyalties are involved is totally unpredictable. His manner became harder.

'Did you like Mr Riddle?'

'No!'

'Did he like you?'

'I shouldn't think so.'

'So why should he do you favours? You strike me as an imtelligent young woman and I refuse to believe that you were silly enough to go to Mr Riddle with such proposals unless you were in a position to either bribe or threaten him.'

Her cheeks were burning now. 'You must think what you like.'

'No. This is a murder enquiry and I want the truth. I said bribe or threaten – which was it?'

Ralph was sitting, staring at the floor, picking at the seam of his jeans. Hilda's jaw was firmly set and she did not open her mouth.

'Did he at any time make advances to you?'

'Certainly not!' She spat out the words.

'Why did you dislike him so much? Would he have been so terrible as a stepfather?'

She hesitated, searching for damaging words. 'He was *repulsive*, oily and ...' She broke off, suddenly calm. 'You don't need to take my word for it, you can ask anybody.'

'Not your mother, obviously.'

She looked up sharply, but suppressed an angry retort.

'I think you tried to blackmail him. What do you know about Mr Riddle which you threatened to make public?'

'Nothing!'

Wycliffe turned to Ralph; in some ways, with his delicate colouring and the readiness with which his cheeks flushed with colour, he seemed more feminine than the girl.

'What do you say to that, Ralph?'

'He's got nothing to say because it's none of his business.'

'But surely he must have been almost as concerned as you were with Mr Riddle's activities, particularly about the fields at the camping site.'

When Ralph spoke his manner was apologetic. 'It's no use, Hilda, we've got to tell him.' He waited for some sign of agreement from her but none came and he went on, 'It was something I found out.'

'What?'

Ralph did not look up. 'I found out that he was visiting Mary Penrose at the house in Moorgate Road.'

'How did you find out?'

'I saw him go in there.'

'Seeing a man go into a house proves nothing against him.'

'He went there every week, sometimes twice. It was obvious.'

'He could well be a friend of the girl's father.'

The boy became sullen. 'I know why he went there.'

'Why were you spying on him?'

'I wasn't!'

'Yet you must have been keeping watch on the house – why?'

The boy was cruelly embarrassed and Wycliffe felt sorry for him.

'Is the girl who lives there accustomed to receive men?'

He hesitated then made up his mind. 'Yes.'

'Were you one of her visitors?'

'Certainly not!'

'Then how do you explain –?'

'I don't explain. I refuse to answer any more questions and you can't make me.'

'All right, we'll leave it at that for the moment, but I may have to see you again.' He turned back to Hilda, who had maintained an air of detachment through the exchanges with Ralph. 'So you threatened Riddle that you would tell your mother about his visits to that house?'

'Yes.' She seemed about to add something but changed her mind.

'Did you?'

'No.'

'If you had done, do you think your mother would have changed her mind about marrying him?'

'Of course, it's obvious.'

Wycliffe reflected how little children knew of their parents. He stood up. He had learned one vital piece of information – where Riddle went on the night of his disappearance – and he had no wish to persecute these youngsters, who seemed to have acted with good intentions.

'If either of you decide that you have more to tell me, you know where to find me.'

He was not displeased. He could add another to the list of places where Riddle might be expected to take off his jacket and tie and relax. Another place where he might have been shot.

He went back to his hotel for lunch and was surprised now that the conference had ended to find a good crowd in the dining-room, which was open to non-residents. They seemed to be local business men and visiting 'reps'. During lunch he listened to animated discussions on the iniquities of British taxation, the necessity for bringing back hanging, indiscipline in schools and the general supine attitude of British politicians. He was tantalised and depressed; he sympathised with their evident frustrations but was appalled by their remedies.

'I sometimes think,' said one of the proponents, 'that what we need in this country is a dictatorship. Somebody who won't hesitate to shoot a few of the troublemakers as a warning to the rest. We'd soon see a difference!'

Of course the dictator would have to be of the right political colour, or he might shoot the wrong people.

For no reason at all his thoughts turned to the girl who lived in the house on stilts. He had a guilty liking for fat girls who laughed a lot and if ever he went off the rails ...

Sometimes he thought how easy it would be to let go, to drift.

'Would you like to finish with a brandy, sir?'

Why not?

The wind was dropping. As he came out of the hotel, prepared for a buffeting, he was aware of the change. It was quiet with occasional strong gusts, the clouds were thinning and soon, with luck, the sun would break through.

When Curtis heard the news he was impressed. 'Mary Penrose! I'll be damned! I wouldn't have believed you could have told me anything I didn't know about the seamy side of life in this town.

'When I was a boy the outfall was still in use and old Penrose was in charge. We had a name for that cove and we used to shout it outside his house until he came out and chased us away.' Curtis's great, moon-like face was softened by recollection.

'Everybody still calls her Mary Penrose but she should be Mary Parkes. She married a chap called Parkes a few years back but he went off and left her. She was better off without him and we weren't sorry to see him off our patch.'

'Form?'

'We pulled him in once or twice for minor offences, but we were pretty sure he was involved in an armed raid in Plymouth. There was nothing we could make stick so he got away with it.'

Curtis sighed. 'I had no idea that Mary was on that tack; she's a nice girl and she's had a hard time what with that husband of hers and now her father almost bedridden with arthritis.'

When Curtis had gone Wycliffe asked the operator to get Sidney Passmore's number and he was put through to a woman who spoke with self-conscious refinement.

'Who is that speaking, please? . . . Yes, my husband is at home . . . Yes, that will be convenient . . . We'll expect you in about fifteen minutes . . .'

Elsie, tightly girdled, answered the door. Her top half was light and frilly; her bottom half consisted of a short, black skirt and plump legs tapering to absurdly small shoes.

'Come in, chief superintendent – have I got that right?'

The Linny was a new and fashionable area and Elsie did her best to live up to it.

'Sidney!'

Wycliffe was received in the lounge, which had a large picture-window looking out to sea. Sidney looked amiable, a little stupid, and very much out of his element. He sat with his legs apart, his hands resting on his knees, and his freckled, rather florid face expressed mild concern.

'You know, of course, that I am enquiring into the disappearance of Jonathan Riddle?'

'Not found him yet?' Sidney spoke conversationally.

'No.'

'It's a queer business. I had no good blood for the man but I wouldn't want anything to happen to him.'

Sidney reached in his pocket and came out with a tobacco pouch.

'Smoke, superintendent?'

Wycliffe caught the flicker of annoyance on Elsie's plump features.

'I heard you were a pipe man,' Sidney said.

Elsie provided a copper ashtray the size of a flower pot.

Wycliffe wanted them to talk. He was prepared to sit there listening, just putting in a remark now and then to keep things moving. He was told in detail of the fields Riddle had bought from under Sidney's very nose and how Riddle then served him with notice to quit.

'I suppose there was a row?'

Sidney smiled sheepishly. 'I told him a few home truths, but it was a waste of breath, there was nothing I could do.'

'He was a *poisonous* man, superintendent,' Elsie said.

'You think he's dead, Mrs Passmore?'

'Don't you? Would you be making all this fuss if you didn't?'

Wycliffe smiled.

'When I think of my former sister-in-law agreeing to marry him, it makes me feel ill, positively *ill*.'

Wycliffe smoked quietly. He was facing the window and seemed to be in a state of dreamy somnolence.

'We can't find out where he was going on Friday evening; you know that he was seen in Albert Terrace, apparently on his way to Moorgate?'

Sidney nodded.

'Of course I've heard the theory that he was going to visit old Jordan.'

'And that Jordan killed him and stuck his body in the Wheel.' Sidney laughed unexpectedly.

'You don't believe that is what happened?'

'Not on your life.'

'Then where was Riddle going?' Wycliffe turned, quite naturally, to face Sidney. 'As far as I can see there is only one house that is easier to get at that way than by going through the town, and that is the house on stilts.'

Wycliffe, watching Sidney closely, saw him stiffen.

'A girl called Penrose lives there with her invalid father ...'

There could be no doubt of Sidney's perturbation; he looked anxiously at his wife and was clearly relieved to see that she appeared unconcerned.

'I expect you know them?'

Sidney made an effort. 'The Penroses? The old man has lived in that house ever since I can remember. He worked for the council and was responsible for the sewage outfall until we had the new drainage scheme.'

Wycliffe changed the subject and the conversation got round to Ralph and his prospects.

'He's a clever boy,' Sidney said, 'but I can't think where he gets it from.'

Elsie frowned. 'He'll be all right if he doesn't start listening to the wrong people.'

'This caravan site of yours, Mr Passmore, is it far from here?'

'Just up the valley a quarter of a mile or so.'

'If you've got a few minutes to spare I would like to see these fields that have caused so much bother.'

Sidney looked astonished. 'The fields?' Then his expression changed and he got up. 'No trouble – delighted.'

'No point in taking the car, we might as well walk.'

Outside Wycliffe said, 'You guessed that Riddle was going to see Mary Penrose?'

Sidney hesitated. 'I must admit that it went through my mind, though I could scarcely credit it.'

'Why not? Did you think that you were the only one?'

He was embarrassed. 'To be honest, I did.' He looked vaguely at the little stream running beside the road. 'It started so innocent like. I used to drop in to have a word with the old man – cheer him up a bit. Well, we got friendly, Mary and me, and it just happened, then it became regular like ...'

'The same night every week?'

'Tuesdays.'

'Riddle went there on some Wednesdays and almost every Friday.'

'I still can't quite believe it.'

'Forgive me for asking, but did you pay her?'

'Not to say pay her, I just helped her out a bit. Poor girl, she's none too well off.'

They walked in silence for a while, then Sidney said, 'I suppose I didn't ought to ask, but it's important to me. How did you find out that I? . . .'

'I had an idea, but I wasn't sure until I saw your reaction when her name was mentioned.'

'Thank God you didn't say anything in front of Elsie!'

'I suppose there's a chance that you might be able to do a deal with Riddle's heirs, whoever they are?'

They reached the caravan site and Sidney paused, resting his arms on the entrance gate.

'I can't see myself doing any better with Sarah and that precious boy of hers than I could with Riddle.'

They smoked in silence for a while, looking over the gate at the well-kept buildings which formed the nucleus of the site.

'Did Mary tell you about Riddle?'

'No.'

'I suppose I've no right to press you.'

'Ralph told me.'

'Ralph!' Sidney looked so astonished that it was almost comic. 'Oh, my God, how did he find out?'

'I should ask him. It's time you and he had a chat.'

'It's bloody difficult.'

Wycliffe turned away from the gate and started to walk back. Sidney fell into step beside him.

'I understand that your brother, Ernie, is staying in one of your vans.'

'Until he can find something more permanent.'

'How long has he been back?'

'Just over a fortnight.'

113

'I suppose you and your brother must know the Riddle family pretty well?'

Sidney was puzzled by Wycliffe's new line of questioning, and Wycliffe himself had only a vague idea of what he was after.

'Ernie and me went to school with Johnny; Sarah was older.'

'The old lady seems pretty fit; does she still get about?'

'She's as active as you or me and a damn sight tougher. It suits her to play the old lady and keep Sarah on a string.' He sighed. 'They're a queer family.'

'The old lady, Sarah, Jonathan, Matthew ... It's a strong strain.'

'Yes, and it goes further back. Old man Riddle was cracked on religion and the old lady's father made a small fortune out of rabbit skins. When he died they found seven thousand pounds in notes hidden away in different places all over his cottage ...' Sidney walked in silence for a minute or two, smoking his pipe and nodding amiably to passers-by, all of whom greeted him.

'Matthew's different; there's a weakness there from his father's side and his uncle knew it. Matthew's father was no match for Sarah. He died young, and perhaps the poor devil was lucky.'

'Sarah seems unnaturally possessive where Matthew is concerned.'

Sidney laughed. 'You can say that again. Like a vixen with only one whelp.'

Wycliffe was trying to get an idea clear in his mind, to focus an image of the family. 'Possessiveness seems to have taken the place of affection with them. None of them shed any tears over Riddle.'

'No, they wouldn't.'

'What about the old lady and Jonathan?'

Sidney paused before answering. 'I doubt if her attitude to Johnny was much different to Sarah's attitude to her boy, but the old lady is a sight cleverer than Sarah; she didn't let it show.'

They reached Sidney's gate and Wycliffe was aware of Elsie's form behind the curtains of the drawing-room.

'Is that all you wanted?'

'For the present.'

Sidney had his hand on the gate. 'I hope it won't be necessary ...'

'I shouldn't think so. Talk to Ralph.'

Chapter Seven

THE UNDERTAKER'S CLOTHES had been found on Tuesday evening, and if the news reached Fleet Street news editors, none of them thought it worth mentioning. By Thursday the finding of the clothes was being linked with the Scapegoat ritual, giving the story an angle, and on Friday three reporters were working through the town's pubs, picking up local colour and gossip. When Wycliffe returned from talking to Sidney he had to give them a statement.

'Isn't it odd that the Wheel has been recovered and not the body?'

'It doesn't seem so to me. At the moment the police have no conclusive evidence that Mr Riddle is dead, but if he is there is no reason to connect his death with the Wheel.'

'You think he might still be alive, naked and shot through the neck?'

Wycliffe did not answer.

The most aggressive of the three, a little chap with a face like a sad clown, said: 'I suppose you've heard what the locals are saying?'

'Surprise me.'

'They're saying that Riddle was gagged and bound, then put into the Wheel while he was still alive – a real Scapegoat. One woman says she heard him scream as the Wheel rolled down the slope.'

Wycliffe still said nothing and the reporter persisted. 'What do you think of that?'

'I think it's nonsense and so do you, but that won't stop you printing it.'

'You're not being very helpful, Mr Wycliffe.'

'I've given you the facts, gentlemen; you can't expect me to do your embroidery for you.'

Wycliffe was talking to them in his little office, where the Salvation Army band had once stored their instruments. There was a notice pasted on the wall above his head: 'Instructions to Bandsmen'.

'A forensic expert was examining the Wheel this morning; did he find anything?'

'I'll know when I get his report.'

Wycliffe was not usually so curt with the press, but he was at a stage in the case when he wanted to be left alone to mull over what he knew and to decide what more he needed to know.

The telephone rang.

'Wycliffe.'

It was Bourne, speaking in a low voice because he knew that the reporters were still with him.

'We've had a report of a body stranded on the shore on the west side of Kernick Head, sir. The man who spotted it says it's inaccessible without proper equipment so Mr Scales is getting through to the coastguards, sir.'

'Good, tell him I'll be with him in a few minutes ... and Bourne, notify Dr Franks.'

He replaced the receiver. The little reporter at once demanded: 'Dr Franks, is he the pathologist?'

'I see you've done your homework.'

'Does that mean that you've found the body?'

'I don't know. A body has been reported stranded on the shore on the west side of Kernick Head.'

In seconds he was alone.

With Scales and Sergeant Conway he was driven to the end of Salvation Street, where the footpath led to the headland; it was not possible to get a vehicle any nearer. As they were getting out of the police car a royal blue Land Rover drew up beside them and a coastguard officer got out.

'I've got the equipment with me and there are three other chaps coming – part-timers.'

They made their way in single file along the cliff path, round the base of the great hump of land which rose steeply to their right. The wind had dropped completely, but there was still a heavy sea running and each wave sent up a sheet of spray as it crashed against the rocks below. The clouds had thinned, the sun was shining and it was almost warm enough to create the illusion of summer. As they rounded the hump and came out on the broad, gentler seaward slope they saw a uniformed policeman standing on the cliff edge, and when they joined him he pointed to the rocky shore below.

The tide had passed its peak and left a mass of debris behind, including the long, bony body of the undertaker, lodged in a miniature gully, apparently wedged between the rocks. The body was naked and horribly mutilated; the black hair emphasised the lividity of the skin.

'That's him all right,' Curtis said. 'Poor bastard!'

Across the cove, about three hundred yards away, the house on stilts looked blindly out to sea, giving no sign of life.

The coastguard officer took stock of the situation.

'It's not going to be easy. I'll get back to my truck; the men should be there by now.'

Wycliffe had scarcely spoken since leaving the hall and Scales knew him too well to try to involve him in conversation.

'Well, I've seen all I want to here, I've got other things to do.' He sounded surly but, at the same time, vaguely apologetic. He waited until the coastguard officer had got well ahead, then followed him along the path back the way they had come. When he reached the Land Rover, which the coastguards were unloading, he acknowledged them briefly and walked on. The three reporters were getting out of a taxi and he raised a hand to them also.

At the end of Salvation Street he paused and seemed to hesitate over whether to return to the town or take the road in the direction of Moorgate and the house on stilts. In the end he turned towards Moorgate. The cove was a sun-trap and as he walked he slipped off his coat and carried it over his arm. When he reached the house on stilts there was still no sign of life; the windows were all tightly shut and the curtains more than half drawn. He left the road at the hairpin bend which would have taken him up to Albert Terrace and followed the path through the kissing-gate to the moor.

The path was narrow and climbed steeply between thickets of gorse which were in flower; nothing to be compared with the dramatic spring show but enough to provide a few patches of welcome colour against the sombre background of the moor in November. As he continued to climb, the sea appeared less troubled and it came as a surprise to see the white turmoil round the foot of each headland and promontory. The sun was getting low over the sea and in an hour or so it would dip below the horizon, where there were horizontal bars of dark colour.

The shed where Riddle's clothes had been found was ahead of him; the land hereabouts was divided into little fields bounded by dry-stone walls, but cultivation had ceased long ago and the fields were choked with bracken and bramble. He looked in the shed but there was nothing except the dank smell of bare, sour soil.

His thoughts were running in circles. 'Matthew Choak is a desperately worried young man. Six months ago, after a seemingly blameless life, he began to steal from his uncle, but he was found out. Cissie Jordan has an illegitimate baby, but she is keeping quiet about the father. Riddle is dead, presumably shot through the neck; his body is naked and mutilated. When he was shot he was not wearing his jacket or tie so presumably he felt at home, wherever it was.' Involuntarily Wycliffe turned to look back at the house on stilts, but it was hidden by a bulge in the slope of the hill ... 'Matthew Choak is a desperately worried young man ...'

The path joined a cart-track leading to Jordan's farm and he could hear a tractor working in the distance. After a moment he spotted Jordan, sitting on his tractor, moving slowly across the sky-line, silhouetted against the setting sun. He picked his way along the edge of the track, avoiding the ruts and pot-holes, which were filled with brown water, and reached the house. The sun was brilliantly mirrored in the front windows. Apart from the noise of the tractor in the distance and the nearby scuffling and squeaking of the rabbits in their cages there was silence. The door was shut and he banged on it with his knuckles two or three times before he heard a movement inside and the door opened. Cissie, her eyes vague and puffed with sleep, looked at him without interest.

He introduced himself.

'Father's out, ploughing.'

'It's you I've come to see.'

She said nothing, but turned and led the way into the living-room, where it was almost dark and the coals glowed bright red between the bars of the stove. A magazine lay on the floor beside a wicker chair where she had been sleeping. The pram was by the dresser but Wycliffe could not see whether or not the baby was in it.

'What's the time?'

'Half-past four.'

She yawned, stretching her arms above her head so that her clothes slid up over her body. 'God! I've been asleep for an hour. He'll be in for his tea directly.'

She picked up a large, enamelled kettle from the fender and went into the scullery to fill it.

'You'd better sit down.'

She came back, put the kettle on the stove, picked up the magazine and placed it on a pile in the window.

'Why are you covering up for Matthew Choak?'

'I don't know what you're talking about.'

'When did you tell him that you were pregnant?'

She shrugged. 'There's no answer to that sort of question.'

'It must have been six months ago, when he started stealing money from his uncle.'

'Stealing? Matthew?'

'With the help of a clerk at the builders' merchants he stole eight hundred pounds from his uncle. Four hundred of it came to him, presumably. How much did he give you?'

Wycliffe was sitting in the wicker chair, the cushions still warm from her body.

'If you don't tell me I shall get it out of him.'

She turned from the stove and looked at him with troubled eyes. 'Do you have to tell my father?'

'Tell him what?'

'That Matthew is ...'

'It's nothing to do with me unless it concerns Riddle's death.'

'If father knew about Matthew he'd want me to marry him. "Give the child a name" – that's what he says.' She nodded towards the pram.

'So why not?'

She looked startled. 'Why not? I wouldn't marry Matthew Choak if he was the last man on earth.'

'But you – '

She cut him short. 'I went to bed with him; that's different. In any case, he didn't want to marry me – afraid his uncle wouldn't approve, which he wouldn't.'

She turned again to the stove and shovelled coal from the scuttle.

'We'd better have a light, I can't see to think.' She reached down a box of matches from the mantelpiece and lit a gas lamp on a bracket near the window. 'Bottled gas. At least it's better than the paraffin we used to have when I was a kid.'

The room came to life in a soft, yellow glow. In the wicker chair in front of the stove it was warm, comfortable and relaxing.

'Did Riddle ever come here?'

'Never. If he had done father would have ...' She stopped herself. 'Father couldn't stand him.'

Wycliffe's head and neck came just above the plaited cane at the back of the chair. There was a clock on the mantelpiece and, above the clock, a small mirror in a gilded frame, darkened by soot. In the mirror he could dimly see the room behind him.

'Did Matthew ever come here?'

'No.'

'Never?'

She sighed. 'A year ago father went to Brittany; he'd been saving up for years and he went on a nine-day excursion. I was here by myself.'

'And Matthew came then?'

'Three times. I'd gone out with him a few times – pictures in Penzance, that sort of thing, and father being away ... Of

122

course, that was when it happened ... You know I worked in Riddle's office?'

If, for example, old man Jordan had come into the kitchen at that moment, Wycliffe might have seen him in the mirror; but what of it? Jordan could come close, take a gun from his pocket and shoot ...

'You are quite sure that Riddle never came to this house?'

'I've told you.'

'Did Matthew ever say anything to you about his uncle?'

She was sitting in a slatted wooden armchair to the left of the stove, her father's chair. The kettle was beginning to sing.

'He used to grumble about him, but it would always end up with the same old story.'

'What story?'

'About him being a partner. "He's bound to do it sooner or later ... If he doesn't do it before the summer I shall tell him what he can do with his job ... I could get a job anywhere ..." You know the sort of thing.'

'Did he ever mention his uncle's will?'

'Not in so many words, but until a month or two back he took it for granted that the business would come to him. He used to say that in a few years his uncle would retire; then he would be in control.'

Bullets are funny things; they rarely do what is expected of them. Sitting where he was, a bullet fired into the back of his neck might pass through and embed itself somewhere in the brickwork above the stove. But a lot depended on the angle at which the shot was fired. If it travelled up into the skull it *might* ricochet off the skull table and bed itself in the bone. If that had happened to Riddle, when Franks performed the autopsy he would find it. If not, then it must be somewhere ...

'Did Matthew ever refer to his uncle's relations with women?'

'No.'

'You know that Riddle was seen in Albert Terrace on Friday evening?'

'Yes.'

'Where was he going?'

'Wherever it was it wasn't here.'

123

Riddle's wound had bled over his shirt collar. If he was shot sitting down there would probably have been blood on the back of his chair ...

He stood up.

'Going?'

He nodded.

She came with him to the door. 'Just as well you're away before father comes in; he likes to gossip.'

'Who do you think killed Riddle?'

He was surprised by her answer. 'Not Matthew, anyway. He might have wanted to but he wouldn't have had the guts.'

The sun had set and dusk was closing over the moor, which looked grey and melancholy.

'It's lonely here.'

'I'm used to it.'

'I suppose your father rarely goes out?'

'Most weeks he's out a couple of evenings – talking to Women's Institutes, Old Cornwall Societies, that sort of thing.'

'But surely he hasn't got a car?'

'They fetch him and bring him back.'

By the time he reached the kissing-gate, it was almost dark. A car with headlights on came towards him, cautiously negotiated the hairpin bend, and for some time afterwards he could hear it grinding up the hill to Albert Terrace. There was a light on in the house on stilts; he could see a faint glow through the curtains of the window on the left of the door.

He had wanted to be sure before tackling Mary Penrose; now he was. He was tempted to go in and get it over, but he had been away from his temporary headquarters for a long time and he did not even know if the body had been recovered successfully. At least there were no lights on Kernick Head, which there would have been if the operation was still in progress. He increased his pace and arrived back at the hall as the church clock was striking six.

Bourne was there.

'Mr Scales?'

'Mr Scales has gone with the body.'

124

'Of course.' For legal reasons, it was necessary to maintain continuity of evidence.

'Anything new?'

'Nothing, sir.'

Bourne's manner seemed even more cold and distant than usual. Was it an unspoken criticism? A detective chief super should immerse himself in bumf until the last trump sounds – and like it.

To hell with Bourne.

'I'm going to get something to eat, then I shall be at the County Hospital with Dr Franks.'

'Very well, sir.'

Before leaving he went into his little office to telephone his wife, Helen.

'It's me ... All right ... The hotel's not bad ... Yes, I had a meal with them last night; they send their love ... You can imagine ... No, I've no idea yet ... Yes, darling ... And you.'

He found Franks in his laboratory, scrubbing up after the autopsy. What was left of Jonathan Riddle had been taken away by attendants to be stored in a refrigerated drawer until the coroner issued his certificate for disposal.

'You remember Tessa?'

Franks's secretary, young, attractive, blonde. Wycliffe said that he did, which was something of a record, for Franks's secretaries came and went with bewildering frequency, though all were to a common stamp. All of them were young, blonde, bedworthy and, according to gossip, bed-willing.

'Would you like coffee?'

'Yes, please, Tessa.'

The electric clock on the wall showed half-past ten; it was dark outside and the slatted blinds were down. The laboratory was lit by a battery of fluorescent tubes, merciless to shadows and propagating a hard, white glare. Franks liked their brilliant unambiguous light, just as Wycliffe preferred a gentle, warm glow with undefined shapes and shadows.

Franks secured his shirt cuffs with gold links, slipped on his jacket and straightened his tie – once more his plump, pink, elegant self.

'He was shot; that's what killed him. All his other injuries, and there are plenty, are superficial and inflicted *post mortem*. It's difficult to be sure, but I'd say he'd been put in the water immediately after death and that he's been tossed about in shallow water over a rocky bottom ever since. The gale would account for it. If he'd been in deep water he wouldn't have been damaged so much and neither would he have surfaced yet, perhaps not for several more days. Decomposition is at an early stage and he's a heavy, bony type with no fat to speak of.'

'How long has he been dead?'

Franks looked at him like a round-eyed baby. 'You should know better than to ask such a question after all I've tried to teach you.'

'How long?'

Franks passed a white hand over his bald head. 'If somebody told me he disappeared some time on Friday night I wouldn't be surprised.'

Wycliffe grinned. 'I wish I could solve my problems by reading the newspapers.'

Tessa came in. 'Coffee.'

They went through to Franks's office, which was not unlike his laboratory except that it was smaller; all white and aseptic, with glaring lights.

'How you manage to work in this beats me.'

'He that doeth truth cometh to the light.' Franks poured three cups of coffee from the percolator. 'Sugar?'

'No thanks.'

'This man Riddle must have had a taste for nuts and raisins; he seems to have eaten quite a few within a couple of hours before his death.'

'Anything else in the stomach?'

Franks screwed up his lips. 'Not much – remnants of an earlier meal which appears to have included ham and tomatoes. The seeds are undigested and he ate the skin.'

'Any ligatures on the body?'

'No. What are you after?'

'Any signs of scorching or burning?'

'No again. Are you taking this Wheel business seriously?'

Wycliffe made a vague gesture but did not answer.

'The day you give something away I'll take a vow of chastity.' Franks opened a drawer of his desk and came out with a polythene bag. 'His watch. For what it's worth, it stopped at twelve o'clock.'

'What about the bullet?'

'Show him, Tessa.'

The girl got up and switched on an X-ray display panel with two plates.

'You see? The bullet was bedded in the left zygoma, lateral to the orbit. It shows signs of spreading, which made me think it must be lead and, therefore, a .22. I've removed it and it's certainly lead, but you'll need an expert to tell you that it's a .22.'

'What about the wound of entry?'

'At the back of the neck, to the right of the fourth cervical vertebra; the bullet passed through the trapezius of that side, grazed the body of the fourth vertebra and proceeded transversely and slightly upwards to the zygoma. The wound of entry was small and I'd say the gun was held at a little more than an inch from the chap's neck.'

Wycliffe nodded. 'Either the gun was canted upwards or Riddle was looking down.'

'But not much, in any case.'

'What about bleeding?'

'By a remarkable chance none of the great vessels was damaged but several minor ones were, of course. There would have been some loss of blood.'

'And the grouping?'

'Group A, rhesus positive.'

'That tallies.'

It is not an easy thing to get rid of a body by dumping it in the sea, except from a boat, Of course it is less of a problem if you have access to a pier or a jetty, but most such places are public and liable to be overlooked, even at night. Inevitably Wycliffe's thoughts were on the basin by the house on stilts. Was it possible ...?

'More coffee?' Tessa was bending over him with the percolator and he got a whiff of expensive perfume.

'Riddle imagined that he was suffering from acromegaly – was he?'

Franks frowned. 'The simple answer to that is, yes. On the other hand, I could find nothing to suggest that his general health was materially affected. He would probably have gone on to a ripe old age.'

Wycliffe drove back and arrived at his hotel just before midnight. There was no night-porter, but he had a key and he let himself in to the deserted lobby. With other notices by the reception desk there was a tide-table and he ran his finger down the column of figures. High tide on the night of Friday, October 30th, was at 23.25.

Chapter Eight

ON SATURDAY MORNING the sun shone, the sea sparkled, colours were sharper and the air seemed fresher. In Wycliffe's temporary office there was only one small, dirty window high up in the wall, but the sun happened to be shining through it and so his desk and chair were placed in a pool of sunlight.

'John Penhaligon, aged 83, retired baker of 14, Prospect Terrace . . .'

There were several reports on his desk but only two of interest. The retired baker had been interviewed in the course of a tedious house-to-house enquiry and now it was a question of whether or not to believe the old man.

'At my age you don't need much sleep by night, and I spend a good deal of time sitting by the bedroom window, smoking my pipe and watching the sea . . . I heard the church clock strike two and some time after that I saw Matthew Choak's little van go by. I thought to myself, "What's he up to at this time of night?" Of course, I didn't know then that the undertaker was missing.'

'How did you know that it was his van; there must be plenty of Mini vans about?'

'I knew because it's got a band of those black and white checks across the bonnet and the roof and running down the back. You know: the things youngsters stick on their cars to make 'em look like racers – but I've never seen it done to a clapped-out old van before.'

'You're sure of the time?'

'I'm sure that it was after two and before half-past, but I can't get closer than that.'

'And the van was going towards the house and not away from it?'

'That's right. As a matter of fact I heard it stop when it reached the house.'

'And it was definitely Saturday night?'

'I'd have said it was Sunday morning if you want it right.'

'Yes, but not *Saturday* morning?'

'Definitely not.'

'Were you sitting by your window earlier in the night, say between eleven and twelve?'

'No, I was in bed asleep.'

'Do you sleep alone?'

'I've been a widower for ten years.'

It was possible that the van had been used to transport Riddle's body, but if so, where had the body been kept for twenty-four hours? Surely not in the house on Buller's Hill?

The other report was from DC Dixon and provided additional confirmation of Matthew's account of his movements on the night his uncle disappeared. A young doctor, making an emergency call in Bal Lane, had seen him trudging home at 2.30 in the morning, looking like a drowned rat.

The telephone rang.

'Mrs Choak is here asking to see you, sir.'

'Bring her in.'

Sarah had spruced herself up; she wore a long, royal-blue coat over a blue dress of some silky material and she had a blue cloche hat pulled down over her straggling grey hair. She came in looking aggressive and clutching her massive black handbag with the brass clasp. 'Oh, there you are! I came because I ...'

'Sit down, please.' Wycliffe pointed to a chair and she sat down, but her manner conveyed the message that she was making no concessions. Wycliffe found himself gazing at the white hairs which sprouted from her upper lip and looked quickly away.

'I suppose you've made up your mind by now that Matthew couldn't have killed his uncle?'

Her eyes darted round the little room, taking everything in.

Wycliffe's manner was judicial. 'If your brother was killed before 2.30 on Saturday morning and if your son's account of

130

his movements is correct, then he could not have killed his uncle.'

It was clearly not the answer she had expected. 'Are you telling me that you still suspect him?'

'Everyone who had a possible interest in your brother's death must expect to be thoroughly investigated.'

'But he didn't get home until half-past two and his car was seen by one of your men at Badger's Cross.'

Wycliffe looked at her with a bland expression but said nothing.

She seemed on the point of making an angry protest, but changed her mind. 'I told you that my brother usually went back to his office on Friday evenings.'

'Yes.'

'That is where he said he spent his time, but it wasn't true.'

'Indeed?'

'Matthew found out three or four months back. Something cropped up, something urgent, and Matthew went to the yard to speak to his uncle about it, but he wasn't there – no sign of him.'

'But that was only one occasion.'

'I've checked since, three or four times, and there's never a light in the offices on Friday evenings.' She pursed her lips and stared at him with her grey eyes. 'He was seeing some woman, like mother said.'

'How do you know?'

'I've got eyes and it's me that had to brush his clothes. I found long hairs – woman's hair, dark brown.'

'But when your mother suggested something of the sort you appeared to know nothing of it.'

She looked down at her hands, sheathed in worn, grey gloves. 'There's no point in stirring up scandal if it isn't necessary.'

There was silence, broken only by the clacking of a typewriter in the hall. It was obvious that she had not yet made her point to her satisfaction.

'They say that Jonathan was last seen in Albert Terrace, is that true?'

'Yes.'

'Going towards Moorgate or coming from there?'

'It was between half-past seven and eight and he was going towards Moorgate, why do you ask?'

'No reason, I just wondered.' She nodded. 'Mother was right, I feel sure of it. He had a regular mistress and he drew out that money to pay her off before he married the other one.'

When Wycliffe at last started to ask questions they were not the ones she had expected.

'Mrs Choak, how long have you been keeping house for your brother?'

'Since Matthew was fifteen, when my husband died.'

'That's more than fifteen years.'

'That's right. Jonathan owed me something for giving up . . . Well, giving up everything, really. After all, I wasn't much over forty, a young woman.'

'What did your husband do for a living?'

'He was a mining engineer and spent most of his time abroad – South Africa, India, Burma . . . I was five years in India with him. It was in Burma that he caught some sort of fever and he never got over it; he came home on leave and never went back.'

She looked down at her handbag and remained silent for a while.

'By rights I should have had compensation, but the firm argued that he was a freelance, working on contract, and their lawyers wriggled out of it. I didn't get a penny.'

She looked at him bleakly.

'Well, thank you for coming, Mrs Choak. I'll bear in mind what you've told me.'

She was reluctant to go. 'Now they've got his body, isn't there some way they can tell when he was killed? I mean, can't they prove that he died before half-past two in the morning?'

'No, I'm afraid not.'

He walked with her to the door of the hall and watched her stepping it out across the square, her shoulders back, her head defiantly erect.

At a little before ten o'clock he was walking along Moorgate towards the house on stilts, smoking his pipe and thinking about Sarah. The house had the same closed, secretive look, its windows tightly shut, the curtains half drawn; no sign of life.

He walked on past the house to the steps and down to the shore. The tide was out, almost at the bottom of the ebb, and a great expanse of weed-covered rocks lay between him and the sea. He stood on the edge of the rectangular basin, which was about ten feet deep, its bottom littered with debris of every description. Now that the tide was out he could see a channel cut in the rocks right out to the tide-line where once the outfall pipe had run. Around the walls of the basin there was a distinct line about five feet from the bottom which, presumably, represented the high-water mark of ordinary tides.

Wycliffe glanced back at the house and again saw the seated figure in the upstairs room, but now he had the impression that the figure was facing him, looking out of the side window. At the same instant he glimpsed a flutter of movement in one of the downstairs rooms. He knocked out his pipe, climbed the steps to the road and walked along to the house. His ring at the doorbell was answered almost at once by Mary Penrose, wearing a flowered housecoat and looking fresh and appetising.

'Oh, it's you.'

He was annoyed, partly by her simulated surprise, partly for a reason which he refused to think about.

'I've been looking at the basin where the sewage tank used to be.'

'Oh? There's been talk on the council of turning it into a swimming pool, but they can't afford it. In any case, father says that it would unusable in rough weather when they most need it. Shall I take your coat?'

'No, thanks, I'll keep it on.'

She led him into a room off the hall, a room which ran the length of the house with a window at each end.

'At least, sit down.'

He sat among the plump cushions of the settee and immediately regretted not taking his coat off. There was a fire in the grate and the room seemed uncomfortably warm. She sat on the settee also, leaving a space between them. The thin woollen dress she wore under her housecoat had a low neck which displayed the deep cleavage between her soft breasts.

There were two easy chairs matching the settee, a television set and a drinks table with bottles of sherry and port and a covered glass dish containing almonds and raisins.

'Is it too early for a drink?'

'Too early for me.'

'Smoke if you want to.'

He felt that she was amused by his ill-humour and this irritated him.

On Tuesday nights Sidney Passmore must have sat where he was sitting and on Fridays, the undertaker. They would sip sherry or port, nibble at the nuts and raisins and allow themselves to wallow in the warm softness. Murmured words, gentle caresses, soothing passionless kisses. For men who needed a mother rather than a mistress.

Was there room for violence amid all this seductive sweetness?

'Excuse me a moment, I've got to put a casserole in the oven.'

She got up and went out; he could hear her doing things in the kitchen. There was a mirror over the mantelpiece and he could see the door in it. His head and neck came above the level of the back of the settee ... He got up and, without much conviction, looked for blood stains on the upholstery. He found none and sat down again. A large, tabby cat came in, sniffed round his shoes then jumped up on his lap. When she came back he was sitting with the cat curled up on his knees.

'You realise that you are guilty of withholding information in a murder case?'

'Me?' She sat down, pulling her housecoat round her.

'Riddle was here on the Friday night he disappeared.'

She did not seem in the least disconcerted. 'So what? I didn't kill him and there was no point in giving them any more to gossip about.'

He just stopped himself from reacting angrily. What was the point?

'Adolph has taken to you – that's an honour, in case you didn't realise it.'

She reached out and stroked the cat's rump, her plump, tapering fingers sinking into the fur.

'Riddle came here every Friday evening, didn't he?'

'Almost every Friday for the past year, and Wednesdays too, some weeks.'

'This last Friday, when did he arrive and when did he leave?'

'About the same as usual; he arrived just before eight and left around eleven.'

'Who was in the house while he was here?'

She looked surprised. 'Father and me; who else?'

'Is your father capable of coming downstairs?'

She shook her head. 'He hasn't been downstairs for over five years. He manages to move about on the level – go to the loo, that sort of thing, but it's all he can do.'

'Do you sleep upstairs?'

'Yes.'

'Did Riddle go upstairs?'

She chuckled, as though the whole thing was a huge joke. 'I see what you're getting at. No, he never went upstairs.' She paused, then added with a grin, 'We managed quite well here.'

'And Sidney?'

She flushed. 'He's different; he started by coming to see father, not me, and he still spends an hour with the old man whenever he's here.'

'Tuesday is his day, isn't it?'

'I see you've been checking up on me.'

'When Riddle was here on Friday evening, did anything unusual happen?'

She frowned. 'It depends what you mean. You know he intended to get married?'

'Yes.'

'Well, he told me that in view of that he wouldn't be coming here any more.'

'Were you surprised?'

'No, I'd expected it; he wouldn't want to start off on the wrong foot.'

'Were you upset?'

'Why should I be? I liked him coming and I shall miss him, but that's all. No strings – that's the attraction as much as anything. Incidentally, he gave me a very nice parting gift – two hundred and fifty pounds.'

'I was wondering if you would mention that.'

'I thought you might be.' She burst out laughing. 'Why play games? I've got nothing to hide.'

'That's not the impression you gave by holding back information from the detective who called on you.'

'I've got nothing to hide, and nothing to tell either. I know nothing about Johnny's death – nothing.'

'Was Riddle impotent?'

The question brought her up short, but after a moment's hesitation she answered it. 'Almost, poor man.'

'What time did you go to bed on Friday night?'

'Right after he left – about eleven-fifteen.'

'Do you sleep in the back or the front of the house?'

'The front. Father's got the bedroom overlooking the sea.'

'Do you sleep soundly?'

She laughed. 'What is all this? I sleep like a log – a clear conscience.'

He lifted the cat off his lap and stood up.

'Going already?'

He said nothing, but walked over to the window which overlooked the sea. The curtains were only a few inches apart and he pushed them aside so that the room was suddenly filled with light. Rocks close under the window were covered with grey and orange lichens; further out they were encrusted with barnacles and beyond that they were blanketed with brown seaweeds, their slimy fronds gleaming in the sunshine.

'The tide's coming in.'

'Yes, it does, twice a day.'

It seemed that she was determined not to take him seriously. Perhaps it was that which made her attractive to a certain type of man.

To the left he could see the rim of the basin.

'Has Matthew ever been here?'

'Matthew Choak? Never, he wouldn't be welcome.'

'But you know him?'

'I went to school with him. I thought he was a nasty little creep then and I still think so.'

He was like a dog sniffing at a weak scent, dodging about,

uncertain in which direction to go. And the girl was laughing at him.

'Did Riddle tell you much about himself and his family?'

'You're asking me for secrets of the confessional.'

He turned from the window to regard her with a cold stare. 'You would be wise to take my questions seriously.'

Her expression became very solemn, but he was sure that he had not made any real impression.

'He told me very little. Like most men he felt that he was hard done by, but he may have had more reason than most ... He found it difficult to get on with people but he wasn't a bad man.'

He walked round the room, examining every object as though it might tell him some secret.

'You were married to a man called Parkes, what happened to him?'

'He cleared out.'

'Why?'

She shrugged. 'I think he'd got himself involved with the law. Don't ask me how, I didn't know and didn't want to. It was a relief to me when he went.'

'Did he have a gun?'

'Not that I know of.'

It was absurd; if Parkes had had a gun it wouldn't have been a .22.

'I would like a word with your father.'

'With father?'

'That's what I said; is there any reason why I shouldn't?'

'Of course not, he'll be delighted to have somebody to talk to.'

She went ahead of him up the narrow stairs, which twisted round. The bedroom had a sloping ceiling and was very simply furnished; a double bed covered with a white quilt, a bow-fronted chest of drawers and the armchair in which the old man sat. It was a swivel chair, and as Wycliffe came into the room he turned from the window to face his visitor.

'It's the detective come to talk to you, father. Mr Wycliffe.'

'Wycliffe? That's an uncommon name, it must have been

an ancestor of yours who translated the Bible into English.'

The old man's chair was placed in a dormer window that was glassed in on three sides.

'He can't move his neck, but with the swivel chair he can face wherever he wants to.'

He was frail and bald; a network of veins showed through the skin of his scalp and his eyes had sunk deep into their sockets, but his voice was firm and there was nothing wrong with his mind.

'I suppose you've come about the undertaker?'

'In a way. I wanted to have a word about the outfall.'

'The outfall? The basin, you mean. You think that's where they pushed him in and you could be right.' He pointed to the binoculars hanging by their strap from the arm of his chair. 'I watched them fishing him out yesterday afternoon and I thought then, "If that's where you've ended up, my friend, I can make a good guess as to where you went in."'

The girl said, 'Well, I'll leave you to it, I've got work to do.'

Wycliffe heard her clattering down the stairs.

'From what I've seen, I imagine there must be about five feet of water in the basin at high tide. Is that right?'

The old man blinked rapidly, which Wycliffe was soon to recognise as a substitute for nodding.

'About that for an average spring – more if there's wind behind it, a good deal less on the neaps.'

Wycliffe sat on the bottom of the bed. 'Can you recall the state of the tide on Friday evening, Mr Penrose?'

More rapid blinking. 'I ought to, I've nothing else to do but watch the water and the shipping. Let me see, the weather was quiet on Friday, misty rain. High tide was about a quarter-past eleven at night, a moderate tide; there would have been between four and four-and-a-half feet in the basin at the top of the flood.'

Wycliffe was fascinated by the view framed by the window; a vast expanse of sea which seemed to shine in its own right with almost dazzling brilliance.

'If a body was placed in the water at that time, would it have been carried away by the tide?'

'Unless it got snagged, certainly.'

'And if it were placed there later – say at three o'clock?'

'On Friday night there would have been no water in the basin after two, not enough to float a cork.'

'What would have been the latest time that the body could have been put in and carried away?'

The old man considered, rubbing his long, knotted fingers over his skull. 'It would be very chancy after one o'clock – impossible, I'd say.'

'So that a body put in later would still be there in the morning?'

'Of course.'

'One more question, Mr Penrose. Is it possible that a body was put in the basin early on Saturday morning and that it remained there until the next high tide without being seen?'

Penrose brushed aside the suggestion with an emphatic movement of his hand. 'Not a chance! The next high was just before twelve noon on Saturday . . .' He broke off. 'As you see, I spend all my time with my glasses, but apart from me there's the coastguard who does his patrol every morning, there are two gentlemen from the town who never miss walking out here for their morning constitutional and on Saturdays, there's the children, off from school . . .' He laughed, exposing discoloured, broken teeth. 'I tell you, Mr Wycliffe, a man's got a job to have a pee on this coast without being seen – during the day, that is.'

Wycliffe thanked him and promised to come again.

'She's a good girl, my daughter, Mr Wycliffe.'

'I'm sure she is.'

'She thinks I don't know what goes on and I don't say anything. What would be the good?'

'I think you're quite right. She's old enough to make up her own mind.'

'All the same, you're bound to wonder whether somebody was trying to make it look . . .' He broke off, in obvious distress. 'All I can say is . . .'

'I think I understand what you are trying to say, and I assure you I take it very seriously.'

Wycliffe lit his pipe as he left the house and walked slowly back towards the town. The weather was quiet and soft again, almost spring-like. He turned down Salvation Street. The door of number sixteen stood open and he could see Laura, on her knees, polishing the linoleum in the front passage. Further along the street a woman was scrubbing her doorstep. It was like going back in time.

Everything seemed to point in one direction, but he was far from happy. For one thing he needed hard evidence, and to get it he would have to show his hand. He climbed the steep slope to *The Brigantine*. The bar had just opened and the only customer was Ernie Passmore, who sat at one of the tables, a huge, freckled hand clasping a pint glass.

'What will you have, Mr Wycliffe?'

'I'll get my own, thanks.' But Wycliffe took his beer to Ernie's table.

'I hear you've been talking to my Hilda and young Ralph.'

Wycliffe got out his pipe and started to fill it. 'I've been talking to a lot of people.'

'But not to me.'

Sober, Ernie was a different man, more like his brother.

'Should I have done? Have you got something to tell me?'

Ernie drank from his glass, wiped his lips and replaced the glass on the table with deliberation. 'Riddle had it coming to him, I'm not wasting any tears over that bastard.'

'I understand that your wife divorced you in order to marry Riddle.'

Ernie hesitated. 'I don't know about that, but it came to the same thing, I suppose. She was going to marry the bugger.'

'And you resented it?'

'I'll say I did! She had her faults but she was too good for him, and what sort of father would he have made for my kids?'

'Did you try to prevent the marriage?'

He looked sheepish. 'Not by killing the bastard.'

'You are very fond of your daughter?'

'She's a good kid and I hope that she and Sidney's boy make a go of it.'

'Did you tell her something you thought she could use against Riddle?'

'No, I didn't.'

'Are you quite sure?'

He looked at his empty glass and shrugged. 'I told Ralph.'

'That Riddle was a regular visitor at Mary Penrose's?'

'Yes.'

'Did you think that that might stop the marriage if your wife got to hear of it?'

'It was worth a try. Women are funny creatures, you can never tell.'

'Did you also tell Ralph that his father was another of Mary's visitors?'

Ernie looked shocked. 'No, I bloody well didn't. What do you take me for?' After a moment he added, 'Anyway, if you knew Elsie as well as I do you wouldn't blame Sidney for getting a bit on the side.'

The whole exchange had been conducted in low tones so that they could not be overheard, but the bar was empty; even the landlord had found business elsewhere and Wycliffe had to rap on the counter when he went to replenish their glasses.

'Where were you the night Riddle disappeared – Friday night?'

'Me? In the pub at Morvyl. I told your chap when he questioned me.'

'Morvyl? What were you doing there?'

Ernie shrugged. 'I've got mates there, the beer's good and it makes a change.'

'You were there until closing time?'

'That's right.'

'And afterwards?'

'I walked home.'

'Alone?'

'No, Joe Steer was with me until we got to the corner of Bal Lane, then he cut through to the terraces.'

'What time did you get back to the caravan?'

'I can't say exactly. Midnight, give or take a bit.'

'Did you meet anybody?'

Ernie looked at him with a sheepish grin. 'Are you checking up on me again?'

'Did you meet anybody?'

'Not to say meet, but Matthew Choak passed me in his old van.'

'Where?' Wycliffe's manner betrayed nothing of his sharpened interest.

'Just after I left Joe, this side of the corner of Bal Lane. He was going like the clappers.'

'Towards or away from town?'

'Away from town.'

'You didn't think to mention this to the detective who questioned you?'

'Mention it? Why?' He looked at Wycliffe in astonishment. 'Christ! You don't think it was Matthew who ...' Ernie scratched his head. 'To tell you the truth it never occurred to me until this minute. I mean, it was Wednesday before you lot started stirring things up and this was Friday ...'

Wycliffe let it go at that.

Chapter Nine

WYCLIFFE WALKED THROUGH the outer office, where the two girls were at work, and into the inner room. Matthew had a drawing board on the table by the window, where he was working on a set of plans. He turned round, startled.

'On the night your uncle disappeared you had a breakdown on your way back from Penzance and you arrived home at half-past two, is that correct?'

He was so nervous that his voice trembled. 'Yes, I –'

'Was the front door locked?'

'Yes, but I have a key.'

'What did you do?'

'Do? I was soaked. I got out of my wet clothes and went straight to bed.'

'Did you speak to anybody – your mother, your grandmother or your uncle?' Wycliffe laid special emphasis on the last word.

'I told you that I didn't see or speak to anybody.' He was a little boy again, defending himself against an accusation, petulant and self-righteous but, above all, scared.

'You went to the bathroom and the lavatory. I suppose you made some noise; did nobody call out, "Is that you, Matthew?" or something of the sort?'

'No.'

'You drove to Penzance, leaving home at about seven-thirty, you went to the film and started to drive back, but your van broke down at Badger's Cross and after trying to start it and sheltering for some time, you walked home, arriving at about half-past two.'

'Yes, I've already told you.'

'Then how do you account for a statement by a witness who

claims that you passed him in your van, driving in the direction of Penzance, at about 11.45 that night?'

'I can't explain it. It's not true.'

The young man was looking at Wycliffe as though he faced the last judgement. Wycliffe had no idea how frightening he could be when his whole personality was concentrated on an interrogation. He never bullied, but his colleagues sometimes said it was because he had no need to.

'Your van is distinctive enough to be easily recognised.'

'I suppose it is, but I wasn't driving to Penzance at 11.45 on Friday night.' Matthew paused as though a new thought had come to him. 'Whoever it was could have made a mistake over the night; I was out at about that time on Saturday night.'

'Going to Penzance?'

'Not to Penzance, no. I was going to Morvyl. At about half-past eleven I had a telephone call – I was in bed but I have an extension in my room for emergencies. It was from the police-man at Morvyl. We had the road up there for some sewer connections and he said that our hazard warning lamps were out. Of course, I had to go over and see to them.'

'Does that sort of thing happen often?'

'Not often. I suppose I get called out, on average, about once a month.'

'Your trip to Morvyl took you along Prospect Terrace, going and coming back?'

'Prospect Terrace? Yes, that's the way I went.' He smoothed his hair back from his forehead and there were little beads of sweat above his eyebrows.

'When did you get back to the house?'

'Just before one.'

'If someone said they saw your van in Prospect Terrace at sometime after two, how would you explain that?'

'After two? That's not possible; I was back in the house by one.'

Wycliffe was sitting back in his chair, watching the young man with calm, unwavering eyes. 'When did you tell your uncle that you were the father of Cissie Jordan's baby?'

Matthew had worked his way round the big desk to the swivel

chair, perhaps to bolster his confidence; now he almost collapsed into it. 'I didn't tell him–'

'But he must have asked you why you needed the money you stole from him. What did you tell him?'

Matthew shook his head from side to side as though trying to make a comprehensive denial. 'I didn't tell him anything, I –'

'But it was to settle with Cissie Jordan that you stole the money?'

He stared down at the desk and spoke in a voice that was barely audible. 'She had to give up her job and she had to buy things. She wouldn't consider getting rid of it . . .'

'Her father must have wondered where the money came from; what did she tell him?'

Matthew smiled weakly. 'He doesn't have a clue, really. Since his wife died it's been Cissie who's looked after everything.'

'You gave her four hundred pounds – your share of what Weekes and you made between you?'

'I gave her six hundred. I made up the difference out of my own money.'

'Wouldn't it have been more sensible to marry her?'

He flushed. 'She wouldn't marry me and, in any case, mother . . .'

'You told your mother?'

He looked up and nodded. 'Mother said it would finish me with uncle.'

Wycliffe left as abruptly as he had arrived. He passed through the outer office, oblivious of the astonished looks on the faces of the two girls. Outside the wicket gate he paused for a moment before setting off along the Backs in the direction of the town centre.

He had to admit that Matthew had come through it very well. The boy would hardly have been stupid enough to invent the tale about the lamps and it was easily possible that Ernie Passmore had been mistaken about the night. Neither was it beyond the bounds of probability that a man of eighty-three had been confused about the time. All the same . . .

Weak – but not vicious. Nevertheless, a weak man, provoked

beyond a certain point, is sometimes more dangerous than one prone to violence.

When he arrived back at the hall Bourne was there alone. Wycliffe stood by the table where the sergeant was making entries on an official form, recording the hours worked by various members of the team.

'Who checked Ernie Passmore's whereabouts on the Friday night that Riddle disappeared?'

Bourne reached for his copy of the case file and referred to the index. 'Section B, statement 8, sir.'

'That's not what I asked you.'

Bourne coloured and turned up the report. 'DC Dixon, sir.'

'Where was he?'

'According to the report he was at *The Morvyl Arms* until closing time, after which he walked home to his caravan at Miller's Bottom.'

'Any confirmation?'

'Yes. The landlord of the pub and one of his drinking cronies.'

'I want you to find out whether he was also at Morvyl on Saturday night.'

Bourne made a note.

'One more thing. I want you to ring the constable at Morvyl and find out whether he complained to Choak on Saturday night about hazard warning lights.'

Another note.

It was extraordinary how, during such a routine exchange between the two men, tension could build up. Suddenly it struck Wycliffe as absurd. 'Have you had your lunch?'

'Not yet, sir. I'm waiting to be relieved by DC Fowler.'

'Good! When Fowler comes we'll go out to lunch together.'

Bourne looked at him sharply but said nothing.

'I'll be in my office.'

Wycliffe took the sergeant to lunch at his hotel and they sat by the great window overlooking the sea, which still sparkled in the sun.

'Have you met any of the people involved in the case, Bourne?'

Bourne was scooping up the soup of the day with precise,

efficient movements – never a drop spilled, never a slurp. He rested his spoon, patted his lips with his napkin and replaced it in his lap. 'Only the two who came to the incident post, sir – Choak and his mother.'

'You've read all the reports?'

'Of course.'

'So what have you decided?'

'Decided?'

'What is your view of the case so far?'

'I haven't got one, sir.'

'Have you discussed it with the men on the ground?'

'Naturally we've talked about the investigation.'

'But you've reached no conclusions, not even tentative ones?'

'No, sir.'

'Yet you expect me to conduct the case and arrive at decisions, even order an arrest, while sitting at a desk.'

Bourne crumbled a bread roll on his side-plate. 'But the situations are not comparable, sir. If you were to adopt that approach you would insist on full and detailed reports from your investigating officers.'

'And don't you get such reports?'

'No, sir. You conduct most of the important interviews and interrogations yourself and afterwards you dictate very sketchy accounts which are only just adequate to keep the files up to date.'

Wycliffe burst out laughing and, after a moment of hesitation, Bourne joined him.

'Anyway, I hope it won't spoil your lunch.'

Bourne topped up his glass from the bottle of Chablis Wycliffe had provided to improve the occasion. 'On the contrary, sir, it's given me an appetite.'

They kept off further shop talk until they were having coffee in the lounge, when Wycliffe said, 'Before you became an administrative officer you did two years as a DC flatfooting around. It's time you got back to it, for the sake of your career.'

'I realise that, sir.'

'Looking forward to it?'

'Frankly, no, but as you say, it is necessary.'

Wycliffe sighed. 'I'm off to Buller's Hill House. You shall come with me and write a model report.'

'I'll do my best, sir.'

As they were walking up Buller's Hill Bourne asked him, 'Why don't you use your car, sir?'

'Because I wouldn't have time to think.'

'By the way, sir, while I was waiting for Fowler to relieve me, I checked with the constable at Morvyl. He did telephone Choak on Saturday night about the warning lamps. I also spoke on the phone to the landlord of the pub at Morvyl. He was quite categorical; Passmore was there on Friday evening from about seven until closing time, but he hadn't seen him for several weeks before then and he hasn't seen him since.'

'This hill is called after General Sir Redvers Buller, the Boer War hero.'

'Really?'

'I had a great uncle who fought under him at Ladysmith.'

Bourne did not quite know what to make of these tender morsels of nostalgic recollection but, believing them to be some sort of test, he held his peace, making no comment.

'This is it.'

They walked up the gravelled drive and Wycliffe rang the front door-bell. There was a delay, but at last it was opened by the old lady.

'Oh, it's you; you'd better come in.'

Wycliffe introduced Bourne.

'Is your daughter not at home?'

'She'll be back around teatime if you want her.'

'In fact it was you we came to see.'

'You're in luck, then.'

She was still an impressive figure, tall, upright, and the bones of her face and skull showed no sign of regression. In many ways she was less marked by age than her daughter and she was certainly a better looking woman.

'In here.'

The drawing-room was gloomier and dustier than he remembered it. A small fire burned on the hearth, giving off more smoke than heat. The old lady sat herself on the red plush sofa and behind her the woodwork of the grand piano gleamed in the dim light. She sat as primly as any Victorian governess. There was a wing-backed chair to the left of the fireplace and she pointed Wycliffe to it.

'You sit here, young man.' She patted the sofa beside her and Bourne sat down, looking puzzled and a trifle apprehensive.

'I hope that my questions won't upset you.'

'I'm too old to be upset.'

'On the night your son disappeared Matthew was late getting back from Penzance because his van broke down.'

'That's what he said.'

'Did you hear him come in?'

'I did. The lock sticks and I heard him turning his key. Later I heard him in the bathroom.'

'How much later?'

'I can't tell you, I think I dozed off in between.'

'How did you know that it was Matthew and not your son?'

'If it had been Jonathan I shouldn't have heard him; he and Sarah were like cats about the house.'

'In any case you have remarkable hearing for a lady of your age.'

'I'm not senile yet.'

'Did you hear anything later in the night?'

'No. What should I have heard?'

'What about Saturday, the following night, when Matthew was called out to see to the lights at Morvyl – did you hear him going or coming back?'

'Both, as it happens. I heard him leaving because I hadn't been in bed very long, and I heard him coming back because I had a bit of indigestion and I couldn't sleep.'

'I don't suppose you know what time he came in?'

'Yes, I had the light on and it was twenty-five minutes past two by my little bedside clock.'

'You are quite sure of that?'

'I shouldn't have said so if I wasn't.'

'What did you actually hear?'

'I heard his key turning in the lock.'

'Nothing else?'

'No, but I can't say that I was paying much attention.'

So the retired baker had been right.

'Where did your son sit when he was in this room?'

'Usually in the chair you are sitting in now.'

'Did he wear a jacket and tie in the house?'

She looked at him curiously. 'When he was in here he was often in his shirt sleeves.'

The back of the undertaker's chair was too high for his head to have come above it.

'If you don't mind we should like to take another look at the upstairs rooms.'

'Help yourselves.'

'You may come if you wish to.'

'No thanks, I've seen them before.' As they reached the door she added, 'We had a certificate from the coroner; the funeral is to be on Wednesday.'

'From the house?'

'Of course.' She captured a stray wisp of hair and tucked it in. 'Sarah has gone to see about getting cards printed, but with the weekend it will be difficult.'

He could not help feeling a grudging admiration for the old lady.

They climbed the stairs past the stained-glass window in the style of Burne Jones. Mahogany doors, mahogany banisters, fretted mahogany in an arch over the landing. Riddle had almost certainly worked in the house when he was a carpenter's apprentice and been impressed. There would have been maids then.

Wycliffe showed no interest in Riddle's study or his bedroom, instead he tried another of the mahogany doors. The old lady's room.

'Look!' He pushed the door open and stood aside for Bourne to see.

A vast wardrobe in walnut, a chest of drawers, a tall-boy and a dressing table with a swing mirror. The great double bed had brass rails and was covered with a patchwork quilt. Here the mustiness which pervaded the rest of the house was replaced by the smell of lavender.

Sarah's bedroom was at the other end of the landing, next to her brother's. A bedroom suite, 1935-vintage, and a little oak bureau. None of the drawers of the bureau was locked but one of the little ones under the lid had been prised open, splitting the wood. Wycliffe lifted out a man's wrist watch and a little wad of letters still in their envelopes and bearing foreign stamps. The letters were written in a thin, spidery hand and each began, 'Dear Sarah', and ended, 'Your loving Matt'. Not to be ranked with the world's great love letters, but probably the most Sarah had ever had. Among the letters there was a postcard photograph of a thin fair man with an indecisive mouth.

Matthew had a smaller room which projected at the back, over the kitchen. A divan bed, a matchwood wardrobe and some shelves by the bed. The extension telephone stood on one of the shelves, between a transistor radio and an alarm clock. There were several dozen paperbacks, mostly science fiction, and, in the wardrobe drawer, Wycliffe found a bundle of 'girlie' magazines and some 'art' photographs of nude girls.

'Are you looking for anything in particular, sir?'

'No.'

After a little while, Wycliffe straightened up and looked at Bourne. 'Are you getting the feel of the place? You and Matthew are about the same age. Imagine yourself in his shoes. He's worked for his uncle ever since he left school, he lives in his uncle's house and this is about all he can call his own. Even here, I expect his mother comes in from time to time and has a good old poke round.'

Bourne looked puzzled. 'What are you saying, sir?'

'I'm not saying anything, I'm trying to understand.'

'He didn't have to put up with it, did he?'

'People are what they are.' Wycliffe shook his head. 'Anyway, you couldn't put all this in a report, could you?'

'No, sir, I couldn't.' He added, after a moment, 'Do you think he did it?'

Wycliffe looked at him with a vague expression. 'How do I know? On Friday night his grandmother heard him come in, because his key grated in the lock. Later – how much later she can't say – she heard him in the bathroom. Had he murdered his uncle in the meantime?'

'In the house?'

'It's possible. A .22 makes only a small crack. If the undertaker had returned after the others were in bed, waited for Matthew, sitting in his shirt sleeves in the drawing-room . . . He would have spoken quietly, "Is that you, Matthew?" Anything could have happened. Of course, if granny had heard the shot it would have been all up, but mother would have covered up for him – to the last.'

'It assumes that he went round armed with a little pistol, or that he knew where to lay hands on one in the house.'

Wycliffe nodded. 'Seems unlikely, doesn't it? Not impossible though. Then there would have been the problem of the body. It couldn't be left there for the old lady to find when she came down to breakfast. It would have to be taken out to the van, and that would certainly have been a job for mother and son, a major job at that. By that time it would have been halfway to low water and too late to dispose of the body in the old sewage outfall that night. Did they leave it in the van for twenty-four hours?'

Bourne was thawing. 'Improbable according to Doctor Franks.'

'But again, not impossible, and Matthew was out at Morvyl seeing those lamps on Saturday night. He said that he got back by one, but the old baker claims that it was after two when he saw the van in Prospect Terrace. Granny says she heard Matthew's key in the lock at about two twenty-five . . .'

'It's a case, sir. Of a sort.'

Wycliffe laughed. 'I'm not sold on it myself. There's another scenario for the house on stilts, one for Jordan's cottage and still another for the house in Salvation Street.'

'Laura Passmore? Surely she's the biggest loser by Riddle's death.'

'On the face of it. The problem is that the man seems to have been shot indoors, somewhere where he felt sufficiently at home to take his jacket and tie off . . .'

152

They went downstairs and the old lady was waiting for them in the hall.

'Well, did you find anything?'

'No.' He just stopped himself from adding, 'We weren't looking for anything.' Instead he said, 'Is there, or has there been, a gun in the house?'

She looked at him in astonishment. 'A gun? If that's what you've been looking for you could have saved yourself the trouble. There's no gun in this house.'

When they left it was clouding over and beginning to drizzle. Fine spells are short-lived in November. They walked down the hill and back to the square.

'Of course, we could put the forensic boys to work in the drawing-room and on the van; we could repeat the operation in Jordan's kitchen, at Mary Penrose's and Laura Passmore's . . .'

'Then why not do that, sir?'

'Because I'm sure that it would be a waste of time.'

As they entered the little hall, two detectives who had been playing cards swept their cards off the table like schoolboys caught in the act. In his office Wycliffe glanced at the morning paper, which had remained unopened on his desk. The case had made the front page; eight column inches in the bottom right-hand corner:

MYSTERY SEQUEL TO CELTIC FIRE FESTIVAL
WAS THE UNDERTAKER A SCAPEGOAT?

He pushed the paper aside. Bourne came in.

'Mr Bellings left a message while we were out, sir. He wants you to ring him before five-thirty.'

Bellings was the assistant chief constable, a suave gentleman, obsessed by statistics.

'Shall I get him on the line, sir?'

'No. Ask them to send me in some coffee.'

Bourne looked at him and Wycliffe thought he saw a faint smile on the sergeant's features. Which was something.

Somebody shot the undertaker while he sat indoors in his shirt sleeves, stripped him of his remaining clothing and pushed him in the sea at the sewage outfall at or near high water. Was that the truth?

A constable brought his coffee and he drank it without noticing. It was always the same when he reached a certain stage in a difficult case. He turned over the facts again and again in his mind until their monotonous repetition affected him like a dull, nagging pain. He would tell himself that he was getting nowhere and become anxious and depressed. Then, more often than not, a way seemed to open. He never believed that it would, for he had no faith. It did not come as a startling revelation – no blinding flash of illumination, only a possibility that he had not previously considered, something that was worth checking.

He sat at his desk, reading reports but not taking in what he read. The same refrain kept going round in his head like an infuriating jingle which refuses to be forgotten: the drawing-room at Buller's Hill House, the kitchen at Jordan's Farm, the sitting-room in the house on stilts and Laura Passmore's living-room. He reached for the case file and turned the pages, reading a bit here and a bit there, out of context and out of sequence. Some passages stood out in his mind with almost photographic clarity, presumably because they had impressed themselves on his mind earlier.

'To the best of my belief the body was placed in the water shortly after death but the possibility that there was an interval of several hours cannot be totally excluded ...' Franks was a cautious man, he always hedged his bets but his hunches were rarely wrong.

A statement from the harbour-master which confirmed the conversation he had had with Mary Penrose's father: 'In my opinion, having in mind recent weather conditions, the finding of the body on the west side of Kernick Head makes it almost certain that the body was placed in the water further to the west, most likely in the neighbourhood of the old sewage outfall ...'

And Wycliffe's own note of his conversation with Penrose: 'There would be no water in the basin after two o'clock, not enough to float a cork ...'

All this gave strong grounds for believing that the body had been put into the sea near the house on stilts about the time of high water on Friday night. That meant within an hour or so of the time at which Mary Penrose claimed that Riddle had left her.

Then there was the inventory of clothing found in the moorland hut and identified by Sarah as that worn by her brother on the night he disappeared: 'Single breasted raincoat, navy blue; grey tweed sports jacket; grey terylene and worsted trousers; grey silk tie ...'

He experienced no sense of exhilaration, no feeling of achievement or of breakthrough, but the jingle stopped repeating itself. He had seen a possible solution, a way in which the conflicting aspects of the case might be reconciled. He left his office, nodded to Bourne as he walked down the hall, and called, 'I'm going out.'

He came out into the darkness of the square; the school playground was on his left. It was ten or twelve feet higher than the square, surrounded by a stone wall with a granite coping and surmounted by a chain-wire fence to stop the children scrambling up and falling over. He did not glance in that direction, but started to cross the square, when there were three shots in quick succession. They were not very loud, like the crack of a fairground rifle, and they had come from behind him, from the playground. He was so astonished that for a few seconds he stood where he was and when he did turn round he could see the top of the wall, the delicate pattern of wire mesh against the sky, and hear running footsteps. That was all.

'Are you all right, sir?' Bourne had come out, unsure whether anything had happened or not. 'I thought I heard shots.'

'You did. Somebody firing from the school playground.' He put a restraining hand on Bourne's arm. 'Save yourself the trouble, lad. There's no way into the playground from the square and by the time you get round by the road, whoever it was will be home and dry.'

He gave instructions for the playground to be searched. If an automatic had been used the cartridge cases should be there. 'Forget about the bullets, we may find them in the morning.'

'Were they firing at you, sir?'

Wycliffe shrugged. 'I was never less than fifty feet from the

155

wall and at that distance, with a small pistol in the dark they'd have had a job to hit a double-decker bus.'

He went back into the hall and telephoned Buller's Hill House. He listened to the ringing tone repeated for more than a minute before he gave up. He turned to John Scales who had just come in. 'John, I want you to go to Buller's Hill House and find out where they all are. If there isn't anybody at home, wait until somebody comes. In particular, I want to know where Matthew is. I'm off to see Mary Penrose.'

'You think it was Matthew?'

'No, but I'd like to know where he is.'

Wycliffe walked along the deserted waterfront. Fine rain was being whisked over the town in little flurries like water from a sprinkler hose caught by the wind. The tide was already clear of the inner harbour and in the near darkness the yellow sand had a ghostly unreality. Somewhere out to sea the beam of the lighthouse appeared intermittently as a misty glow in the sky and the fog-horn was sounding.

He walked in the direction of the headland, turned up Salvation Street, then right, along Moorgate, to the house on stilts.

It was eight days almost to the minute since the undertaker had arrived at the house on stilts and rung the doorbell for the last time. He had two hundred and fifty pounds in his pocket with which to pay off his mistress in preparation for the taking of a wife. Although it was dark and the road twisted away in both directions, the undertaker had stood still and listened for several seconds before venturing up the steps to the front door.

Wycliffe rang the doorbell. A subdued glow came through the curtains of the window on his left.

'Who is it?' Her voice sounded anxious.

'Superintendent Wycliffe.'

She had been watching television, another of those comedies where the audience laughs immoderately at thin jokes.

'I couldn't think who it was. Take your coat off.'

'No, I'm not staying.'

He followed her into the sitting-room, where she cut the sound on the television but left the picture.

'Sherry?'

'No, thanks. When Riddle came here last Friday night I suppose you let him in and took his coat?'

She looked surprised. 'Why, yes –'

'What sort of coat?'

'A raincoat, a greyish-coloured raincoat.'

'Not navy blue?'

'No, I know he's got a navy blue one but he wasn't wearing it on Friday night.'

'You are quite sure?'

'Positive.'

'What about his jacket?'

'His jacket?'

'A sports coat, wasn't it?'

'No, he was wearing a suit, a light grey suit.'

'Did you notice his tie?'

She smiled. 'As it happens, I did. It was one I gave him – a bit loud, a sort of burnt orange. I know he hated it, but he wore it to please me.'

'You are sure he was not wearing a grey silk tie?'

'Quite sure.'

She had on her housecoat, which offered a fair display of bosom, and Wycliffe wondered how long it would be before she found a successor for the undertaker.

'When he left, did you go to the door with him?'

'No, he liked to let himself out – quickly, for fear of being seen. Poor man, he was terrified that somebody might find out that he came here.' She laughed as though it was all one big joke.

'After he'd gone, did you hear anything?'

'What sort of thing?'

'Anything unusual.'

'No, I don't think so, nothing I remember.'

'Thank you, that's all. Give my regards to your father and tell him not to worry.'

'Why should he worry?'

'Just a figure of speech.'

'You're a funny man.'

She came with him to the door, and the light from the hall cut an orange path across the roadway.

'You want to watch out, or people might get the wrong idea about you.'

Chapter Ten

SCALES NOTICED THE change in him but did not remark on it. 'They've found two of the cartridge cases so far, sir.'

'That will do, send them to forensic.'

'A .22 automatic.'

'Yes, and I'll bet it's got a mother-of-pearl inlay on the butt.'

'Sir?'

'Never mind.'

'I went to Buller's Hill House and Sarah opened the door to me. She said that she had heard the telephone ringing but she was in the bath.'

'What about her mother?'

'Out visiting. A Miss Uren who is as old as she is and lives in Harbour Terrace, the one below Bay View.'

'And Matthew?'

Scales frowned. 'That's the interesting one. According to Sarah, he's in Penzance to keep an appointment with Bryant, the builders' merchant. Sarah was a bit cagey, but it seems that Bryant is considering putting in a bid for the business when it comes on the market and he wanted some information from Matthew about its scope and potential.'

Wycliffe nodded.

'If that's true, it couldn't have been Matthew who took those pot shots at you.'

'Nobody took any pot shots at me.'

'Somebody fired three shots.'

'That's not the same thing.'

Scales dropped the subject. 'Shall I ring Bryant and check?'

'There's no need. Sarah was telling you the truth.' He added after a moment, 'I've been very stupid about this one, John.'

They were standing in the little Salvation Army Hall which looked even more shabby and desolate in the light of unshaded electric lamps. Bourne was sitting at his table engrossed in a mound of paper; DC Fowler was typing at another table.

'I've forgotten where I left my car, John; I haven't used it lately.'

'Mine is in the yard behind the nick.'

'Good! Perhaps you will run me up to the house.'

'The house?'

'Buller's Hill.'

The next two hours would remain in Scales's memory for a very long time to come and would become part of the folklore of the force.

'It wasn't anything he said or did, it was the atmosphere he managed to create . . .'

If Wycliffe had heard those words he would have been astonished. His comment to his wife when the case was over was, 'That family . . . the atmosphere in that house!'

The car climbed the steep hill through a curtain of misty rain. As they neared the top the headlights picked up the gloomy laurels and the gable which rose above them. They left the car outside the gate and crunched over the gravel to the front door. Wycliffe rang the bell. There was a light in the hall and another in the sitting room; Sarah came to the door.

'What a time to come! Can't you come back in the morning?'

Wycliffe did not answer; he merely stood there until she moved aside to let him in.

'Mother's having her cocoa before going to bed.'

The old lady was sitting erect on the plush sofa, a mug clasped in both her bony hands.

'Well?' Sarah bent over the fireplace and poked the dying fire.

'I would like to see your brother's clothes.'

She still had her back to him, tidying the hearth. 'His clothes? What, especially, did you want to see?'

'A jacket which matches the trousers found in the shed, a greyish raincoat and an orange, woollen tie.'

'I gave all that away with some other things of his.' She turned to face the room and Scales could have sworn that her lips

160

twitched in the hint of a smile. 'A woman came to the door asking for jumble and I was going to give her the lot until it occurred to me that Matthew might make use of some of it.'

The old lady was sitting on the sofa, still clutching her mug, her eyes moving from Wycliffe to her daughter and back again. She was a spectator, determined to miss nothing.

'If I were you, mother, I should go to bed; you've had a tiring day.'

'I'll go when I'm ready.'

Sarah sat in the armchair, her hands resting in her lap, apparently relaxed. The blue, silky dress she wore hung limply over her bony knees, her grey stockings sagged over her ankles and her shoes were scuffed at the toes.

Wycliffe watched her with a dreamy expression. 'I suppose your husband gave you the little pistol when you were abroad and you've kept it all these years.'

'I've no idea what you are talking about.'

'You've been carrying it about with you in your handbag. It may still be there for all I know, but whether it is or not, we shall find it.'

The black bag with its great brass clasp was by her chair and, at a sign from Wycliffe, Scales went over and picked it up. He opened the bag, looked inside, then with a handkerchief cautiously lifted out a small automatic, holding it by the muzzle. It was little more than a toy, dangerous only at close range; the sort of weapon empire-builders on lonely outstations gave to their wives. Wycliffe saw with a flicker of amusement that the butt was inlaid with mother-of-pearl. Sarah's face was expressionless but her mother looked at her in utter astonishment.

'We can show that the gun has been fired recently and later, when you come to the station, a paraffin test will prove that it was you who fired it.'

There was a longish silence during which they could hear the clock ticking in the hall and the muffled sound of the foghorn on the lighthouse. So far Sarah seemed unimpressed; she sat back in her chair showing neither interest nor concern. Scales thought that she seemed to be listening for something, and it occurred to him that it must be for the return of her son.

Wycliffe took his pipe from his pocket and with a gesture, asked for permission to smoke. It was the old lady who gave it, with unaccustomed graciousness. 'Smoke, by all means, Chief Superintendent.'

He started to fill his pipe. 'Gossip in this town allows of few secrets, but one of the better kept ones was your brother's association with Mary Penrose. However, you knew of it, for when you came to see me you hinted at such a relationship and implied that it might be connected with his death.

'Your main concern was to ensure that Matthew could not be accused of the murder of his uncle and Friday night, as it happened, offered a combination of circumstances which might not have occurred again. Your brother was visiting his mistress, the tide was right, it was the day before the Wheel ceremony and your brother had recently antagonised a number of people. Above all, Matthew was well provided with an alibi.'

He put a match to his pipe, drawing on it in short puffs. 'What you did was extraordinarily well-planned and carried out with a resolution which I find astonishing.'

For the first time Scales detected some response. Sarah pulled down the uneven hem of her dress and settled back in her chair. The old lady sat like a carved image, not moving a muscle.

Wycliffe's manner became more conversational; he, too, sat back in his chair, drawing comfortably on his pipe. 'Your brother must have been very surprised to find you waiting outside the house on stilts. It was after eleven o'clock, a misty night, and you probably startled him, for he was very nervous ... Did you pretend that you were there by chance?'

Sarah's grey eyes were on him and for a moment Scales thought that she was going to answer the question, but she did not speak.

'It doesn't matter; you don't have to answer questions. In fact, I'm supposed to warn you about saying anything.' He rattled off the official caution. 'Anyway, your brother's main concern would have been to get out of earshot of the house and that suited you.

162

'A hundred and fifty yards beyond the house, before one reaches the hairpin bend, the cliff drops to the shore in two stages; a five or six foot drop to a grassy platform, then a descent to the basin of fifteen or twenty feet. It was there that you acted. It was not difficult, for you are nearly as tall as your brother.'

Sarah showed some interest now, but she might equally have been listening to *A Book at Bedtime* on the radio.

'You were on his left; he was between you and the drop; you had your pistol in your right hand. All you had to do was to bring it up to his neck and fire; a gentle push and he would roll down to the plateau.'

Wycliffe stopped speaking but nobody moved. Scales looked at Sarah; her features were composed and the only word he could think of to describe her was *complacent*. They sat for a time like huge wax figures in a tableau. Most of the light from the huge copper electrolier was lost in the dark walls and woodwork, so that much of the room was in shadow.

In the silence they heard a car climbing the hill in low gear and it was obvious that Sarah was listening intently. The car reached the top of the hill, the engine changed its note and the car moved off along Prospect Terrace. The old lady stooped and placed her empty cocoa mug on the carpet by her feet; then she sat back on the sofa, her hands clasped in her lap and her eyes on Wycliffe.

Wycliffe sat looking at Sarah; his expression was bland, contemplative, and his posture relaxed. 'I suppose you waited a while, looking back at the house in case somebody had heard the shot, but all was quiet. Your next job was more difficult, but there was hardly any risk. Moorgate is little used at any time and the chances of somebody coming by after eleven at night are small, but even if a car did pass, the body was well below road level and all you had to do was crouch beside it.'

He turned to Scales. 'It really was exceptionally well conceived and carried out.'

Most killers are inordinately conceited and Scales knew that Wycliffe was using flattery to break down the woman's resistance.

'You set about undressing the body. It was difficult, but you are a powerful and resourceful woman. You succeeded. You had

163

a bag with you in which you put his clothes and when you had finished you simply rolled his body over the edge and it fell into the basin, into about five feet of water.'

Scales had been a policeman for fifteen years and he was by no means a sentimentalist, but he found it difficult to believe that one of these women was the mother and the other the sister of the murdered man. At some time in the past, when Riddle was a little boy, his big sister, seven or eight years older, must have looked after him, mothered him, perhaps pretended to herself that she *was* his mother. Looking back on her life, her marriage must now seem like an interlude spent away from 'home', the home she had shared with her mother and brother, and later with her son. Surely there must have been sentimental moments, shared nostalgic memories . . .

The pile of glowing embers in the grate suddenly collapsed and one smouldering coal rolled out into the fender. Wycliffe got up to retrieve it and threw it back on the fire. The clock in the hall struck eleven, doling out the strokes with seeming reluctance.

It seemed to Scales that Wycliffe was marking time, waiting.

'If the girl in the house on stilts had killed your brother she would not have left his body within a stone's throw of her front door; she would almost certainly have disposed of it as you did. But you stripped his body naked and you had more than one reason for doing so. You wished to guard against the remote possibility that it would not be found, so you retained sufficient evidence to allow a presumption of death. But that was not your only reason.

'Anyway, with your bag of clothing you set out for home, and the remaining risk was that you might be seen returning to your house very late at night. I don't know what you actually did, but the Ordnance Survey map shows a footpath which goes round the back of Bay View Terrace and passes your back gate. Realising how meticulously you went to work my guess is that you took that path. You let yourself in by the back door and went to your room. I have noticed how quietly you move.'

She was smiling, there could be no doubt of it, and Scales was sure that she was about to say something when they heard again the sound of a car climbing the hill. This time they all stopped to listen and they heard the car turning in at the gate and the crunch of its wheels on the gravel. Sarah got to her feet, but Wycliffe said quietly, 'Please stay where you are, Mrs Choak.'

She sat down again without protest.

They heard the car door slam, footsteps on the gravel, then Matthew's key in the lock. Wycliffe went to the drawing-room door and stood while the young man took off his outer coat.

'Come in and sit down.'

Matthew came to the door and stood blinking in the light, looking from Wycliffe to his mother and back again.

'Do as he says, Matthew, and say nothing – *nothing*, do you understand?'

'Yes, mother.'

He had a slight unaccustomed colour and Wycliffe wondered if he had been drinking.

They settled once more; Matthew sat on the sofa next to his grandmother.

Wycliffe turned again to Sarah. 'You wanted to put the clothes somewhere where they were sure to be found without in any way implicating you or your son. You also wanted to suggest that the crime had been committed in circumstances of some intimacy. Your solution to this problem was of a piece with the rest of your planning. By removing the bloodstained raincoat, jacket and tie and substituting others you immediately conveyed the impression that your brother had been shot indoors, in a state of semi-undress, and you knew that this would implicate the Penrose girl. All you had to do was to say that the clothes found were those your brother had been wearing when he left home on Friday night. Who would question your word?'

Matthew opened his mouth to speak but his mother was too quick for him.

'Matthew!'

'On the Saturday night you carried the bag of clothes, including the substituted items, to the shed on the moor, knowing that it would be found by somebody, perhaps by the police in their search for your brother. It was just what Mary

Penrose might have done if she had been guilty, and you rightly assumed that it would look like a clumsy attempt to implicate Jordan, with all the subsequent tomfoolery about the Scapegoat and the Wheel.'

Wycliffe paused to relight his pipe. 'Well, Mrs Choak, whatever else you have done, you have certainly made a place for yourself in the history of criminology.'

Sarah could scarcely resist preening herself, and her pursed lips trembled on the verge of a satisfied smile.

'You had taken a great deal of trouble to protect your son from suspicion, but perversely, I continued to treat him as a principal suspect and you felt compelled to act. You came to see me and pointed out how irrational my attitude was and offered a broad hint about your brother's association with Mary Penrose. When that failed you tried something more dramatic. This evening, while Matthew was keeping an appointment in Penzance, you fired three shots – not at me, but close enough to make your point. Here was the killer, attempting another crime with Matthew safely out of the way.' Wycliffe shifted in his chair so that the springs creaked. 'It was a mistake.'

He looked at Sarah as though seeking her agreement, and Scales saw a barely perceptible nod.

There was a long silence. The old lady was watching her daughter, and once she opened her mouth to speak but changed her mind. Matthew sat beside his grandmother, his body bent forward, his hands clamped between his knees as though trying to make himself as small as possible. The unnatural colour had gone from his cheeks and he looked ill.

It was Sarah who eventually broke the silence. 'All right, I'll come to the police station with you and give you your statement, then we can watch the lawyers fight over it.' She spoke almost with relish. 'I suppose I'm allowed to go upstairs and put a few things together?'

Wycliffe shook his head. 'We haven't got to that stage yet.' He took his time before speaking again and when he did it was to Matthew, not to Sarah. 'You didn't hear the whole story, Matthew, but you heard enough to know that your mother has confessed to murder.' The use of the Christian name and his

166

fatherly tone took them all by surprise. Matthew looked up momentarily but said nothing.

'Do you think that your mother is a murderess?'

Matthew did not answer.

'Do you?' His manner was coaxing. 'You're not a child; you're a man on the wrong side of thirty. You must have some views and opinions of your own. Do you think that your mother took her little gun and shot your uncle as he came away from his mistress?'

'I don't know.'

'You've no right!' Sarah was white and tense. 'I've told you; I've admitted everything; what more do you want?'

Wycliffe did not even glance in her direction but turned to her mother. 'What about you, Mrs Riddle? Do you believe that your daughter murdered her brother? You're a shrewd woman, you sit and watch what goes on. I'm sure you must have your own ideas.'

For once the old lady was taken aback. She looked up at Wycliffe and though her lips moved no words came. Then, with an effort, she regained control and muttered, 'I didn't know she had a gun.'

Finally he returned to Sarah. 'It puzzled me at first why you went to such lengths to protect your son from mere suspicion. For a woman of your intelligence it seemed out of character.'

Sarah put on a show of angry indignation. 'I don't know what you are trying to do unless you want to humiliate me.'

Wycliffe went on as though she had not spoken. 'Then the explanation occurred to me and when it did, it fitted with other evidence. I think that my account of what you did was correct except in two important particulars; you did not kill your brother and you did not place the bundle of clothes in the hut on Saturday night, though it was put there at your direction.' He turned his eyes on Matthew, who was staring at his shoes. 'What have you got to say to that?'

Matthew gave no sign that he had even heard the question, but his mother was desperate. 'Take no notice of him, Matthew. He's talking nonsense and he knows it.'

'Your mother was so protective because she knew that it was

you who had killed your uncle and she was afraid that under any real pressure you would admit it.' He paused for a moment then added, 'And she had good reason to be worried.'

The old lady was looking at Wycliffe in amazement. 'You mean after all that it was –'

Sarah's voice, brimming with hatred, cut across her mother's words. She spoke through her teeth and her hands were clenched. 'You keep out of this! Keep out of this or, by God, I'll . . . ' Emotion choked her words.

Wycliffe still continued as though nothing had happened. 'It was you, Matthew, who waited outside the house on stilts; you waited there with the little pistol you had stolen by breaking open your mother's drawer. I don't think you went there with the intention of killing your uncle; you wanted to intimidate him, perhaps to blackmail him with the knowledge you had of his association with Mary Penrose.

'But your uncle was not easily intimidated. He had nothing but contempt for you and your threats and he expressed himself in words which were as humiliating and wounding as he could make them. It was not the first time that he had spoken to you in that way, but this time you had a weapon. The anger, hatred and frustration that was in you could, at last, find an outlet. It was irresistible. You shot your uncle and the body rolled off the road down to the little grassy plateau below. Horrified, and scared almost out of your mind, you rushed home to tell your mother what you had done.'

Matthew, who had been sitting as though petrified, began to tremble. His whole body was shaken by convulsive spasms then, suddenly, he jumped up and blundered out of the room. Sarah would have followed, but Wycliffe snapped at her to stay where she was and it was Scales who went after him. They listened to pounding feet on the stairs, a door slammed and there was silence.

Sarah turned on him. 'Now see what you've done with your lies!'

Wycliffe's response was mild. 'He'll be all right, Mr Scales will look after him.'

For the first time since he entered the house, Wycliffe seemed really to relax. He knocked out his pipe in the grate, refilled and lit it; during this lengthy operation the two women neither moved nor spoke. The old lady was looking at her daughter as though seeing her for the first time, and Sarah herself was staring at nothing, her hands clasped tightly together in her lap.

When Wycliffe spoke his manner was calmly reasonable, almost consoling. 'You've known from the start that if we were ever in a position to put real pressure on your son he would crumble, and every move you made was aimed at shifting suspicion from him to somebody else – anybody else, eventually yourself.

'I said that you were a resourceful woman and that is certainly true, but in reconstructing the crime just now I remarked on your planning; in fact, there was no planning, no long-term planning anyway. Though much of the evidence pointed to a premeditated and carefully thought-out crime, the actual killing was the result of an outburst of uncontrollable rage on the part of a rather weak young man against the humiliating contempt of his uncle. Your part in it was improvisation.'

Wycliffe stared at the glowing bowl of his pipe. 'Faced with your son's terrible confession, you acted at once; you sent him off in his van, primed with the story of the film and the breakdown. You had the foresight to make him *act out* as much of the lie as possible.'

'It was no lie, it was the truth!' Sarah protested, but her words carried no conviction.

Wycliffe shook his head. 'It's no use. We have a witness who saw him driving out of the town on the Penzance road after half-past eleven on the night your brother disappeared.' She did not argue and he went on, 'With Matthew out of the way you set about disposing of the body and you brought the clothes home with you, intending to use them in some way which would divert suspicion. Sometime during the next twenty-four hours you hit on the idea of replacing the raincoat, jacket and tie, which were bloodstained, with others which were not.

'Then, either by accident or design, it happened that Matthew went to Morvyl on Saturday night to see to the lamps, and you gave him the clothing and told him what to do. He says that he was home before one o'clock but we have a witness who saw his van in Prospect Terrace after two. He had ample time to visit the hut on the moor.'

Wycliffe got up from his chair and stood with his back to the fire, which was now almost out. 'You know that it's all over now. With the information we have, Matthew wouldn't stand up to five minutes' close interrogation, and in his own interest it would be better for him to volunteer a statement.'

When Sarah spoke all the fight had gone out of her; she looked grey and tired. 'Can I speak to him?'

'Of course. You can go upstairs now, if you want to.'

'Can I see him alone?'

Wycliffe hesitated, then saw the look in her eyes and nodded. 'Very well.'

He followed her up the stairs and knocked on the door of Matthew's room before going in. Matthew was lying on the divan, curled up like a child, his knees almost up to his chin. Scales, getting up from a cane-bottomed chair, shrugged. 'He's said nothing.'

Wycliffe muttered, 'Leave them alone but wait outside.'

Sarah hesitated in the doorway for a moment before going in and closing the door behind her. Wycliffe went slowly downstairs and back to the drawing-room where the old lady had not moved from her place on the sofa.

'I've left them together.' He picked up his pipe, which he had left on the mantelpiece.

'I can't get over it. I wouldn't have thought he had it in him.'

Wycliffe said nothing; he was looking at a framed photograph on the mantelpiece. It was of a younger Sarah – thirty years younger. She sat in the photographer's studio with her baby on her lap. A good looking, determined young woman; nobody's fool.

He turned to the old lady. 'What will you do now? Is there somewhere you can go?'

She looked at him in surprise. 'Go? Why should I go anywhere? This is my house, isn't it?'

THE END

available from
THE ORION PUBLISHING GROUP

Wycliffe and Death in Stanley Street
£6.99
W.J. BURLEY
978-0-7528-4969-0

Wycliffe and the Scapegoat £6.99
W.J. BURLEY
978-0-7528-4971-3

Wycliffe in Paul's Court £5-99
W.J. BURLEY
978-0-7528-4932-4

Wycliffe and the Quiet Virgin £5.99
W.J. BURLEY
978-0-7528-4933-1

Wycliffe and the Tangled Web £6.99
W.J. BURLEY
978-0-7528-4446-6

Wycliffe and the Cycle of Death
£5.99
W.J. BURLEY
978-0-7528-4445-9

Wycliffe and the Last Rites £5.99
W.J. BURLEY
978-0-7528-4931-7

Wycliffe and the Guild of Nine
£5.99
W.J. BURLEY
978-0-7528-4384-1

Wycliffe and the Pea-Green Boat
£6.99
W.J. BURLEY
978-0-7528-8186-7

Wycliffe and the School Bullies
£6.99
W.J. BURLEY
978-0-7528-8085-3

Wycliffe and the Beales £5.99
W.J. BURLEY
978-0-7528-5872-2

Wycliffe and the Winsor Blue £5.99
W.J. BURLEY
978-0-7528-5873-9

Wycliffe and Death in a Salubrious
Place £6.99
W.J. BURLEY
978-0-7528-6535-5

Wycliffe and the Four Jacks £5.99
W.J. BURLEY
978-0-7528-4970-6

Wycliffe and the Dead Flautist £5.99
W.J. BURLEY
978-0-7528-6490-7

Wycliffe's Wild-Goose Chase £5.99
W.J. BURLEY
978-0-7528-6491-4

Wycliffe and How to Kill a Cat
£5.99
W.J. BURLEY
978-0-7528-8082-2

Wycliffe and the Guilt Edged Alibi
£6.99
W.J. BURLEY
978-0-7528-8083-9

Wycliffe and the Dunes Mystery
£6.99
W.J. BURLEY
978-0-7528-8185-0

Wycliffe and the Three-Toed Pussy
£6.99
W.J. BURLEY
978-0-7528-8084-6

All Orion/Phoenix titles are available at your local bookshop or from the following address:

Mail Order Department
Littlehampton Book Services
FREEPOST BR535
Worthing, West Sussex, BN13 3BR
telephone 01903 828503, *facsimile* 01903 828802
e-mail MailOrders@lbsltd.co.uk
(Please ensure that you include full postal address details)

Payment can be made either by credit/debit card (Visa, Mastercard, Access and Switch accepted) or by sending a £ Sterling cheque or postal order made payable to *Littlehampton Book Services*.
DO NOT SEND CASH OR CURRENCY.

Please add the following to cover postage and packing

UK and BFPO:
£1.50 for the first book, and 50p for each additional book to a maximum of £3.50

Overseas and Eire:
£2.50 for the first book plus £1.00 for the second book and 50p for each additional book ordered

---

BLOCK CAPITALS PLEASE

name of cardholder _____   *delivery address*
                     _____   *(if different from cardholder)*
address of cardholder _____   _____
_____   _____
_____   _____
_____   _____
     postcode _____   *postcode* _____

☐ I enclose my remittance for £_____

☐ please debit my Mastercard/Visa/Access/Switch (delete as appropriate)

card number ☐☐☐☐☐☐☐☐☐☐☐☐☐☐☐☐☐☐

expiry date ☐☐☐☐   Switch issue no. ☐☐

signature _____

prices and availability are subject to change without notice